The Brahmin

Ravi Shankar Etteth is the author of seven novels: *The Tiger by the River* (2002), *The Village of the Widows* (2003), *The Gold of Their Regrets* (2009), *The Book of Shiva* (2016), *The Brahmin* (2018), *Killing Time in Delhi* (2019) and *Return of the Brahmin* (2021). He has been a graphic designer, political cartoonist and editor of magazines and newspapers. He lives in Delhi and works as a consulting editor with The New Indian Express Group.

The Brahmin

Ravi Shankar Etteth

First published by Westland Publications Private Limited in 2018

Published by Westland Books, a division of Nasadiya Technologies Private Limited, in 2023

No. 269/2B, First Floor, 'Irai Arul', Vimalraj Street, Nethaji Nagar, Allappakkam Main Road, Maduravoyal, Chennai 600095

Westland and the Westland logo are the trademarks of Nasadiya Technologies Private Limited, or its affiliates.

ISBN: 9789357761376

10 9 8 7 6 5 4 3 2 1

Typeset in Bembo Std by SÜRYA, New Delhi
Printed at Nutech Print Services-India

For C: Someday.

Contents

Cast of Characters

ASHOKA: The ruler of the Magadha kingdom

ASANDHIMITRA: The queen of Magadha

THE BRAHMIN: Ashoka's Head of Secret Service

HAO TRAN: The Brahmin's assistant

LORD SUMA: Kalingan spy who is also the ambassador to Magadha

MUR: Suma's beautiful niece

RADHAGUPTA: Ashoka's prime minister

ANTOCHLIUS: Greek soldier and spy

AEIMNESTUS: Soldier in Alexander's army and father of Antochlius

KALANOS: Brahmin seer and Alexander's friend

TELEMACHUS: Renegade Greek mercenary

CHIEF EUNUCH: Guardian of the harem

DEVAVARMAN: Viceroy of Ujjain

ASA: Asandhimitra's nurse

Murder in the Harem

267 BC

Pataliputra: The capital of the Mauryan kingdom

'Someone is killing my concubines,' King Ashoka roared. 'And you do nothing, Brahmin?'

Ashoka's feared spymaster stood before his liege with an inscrutable expression on his smooth, golden-skinned face. His hooded, expressionless eyes surveyed the monarch without flinching. Ashoka's hands clenched and unclenched as if throttling an invisible foe, his chest heaving beneath his loose cambric robe in frustration. The Brahmin knew it was going to be one of those days.

They were in the royal garden, where Ashoka's large frame occupied most of the gilded wooden bench under the tree that bore his name. The scent of flowers perfumed the falling dusk. Six slave women stood around the king, gently waving fans made of peacock feathers. Their shapely legs were wrapped in scarlet silk embroidered with gold, and strips of the same fabric bound their perfect breasts. The Brahmin thought of the dead concubine, the stench of her charred flesh, and the deadly token beside her corpse. He sighed.

It had happened like this. One of the his spies had discovered a concubine's corpse in a cremation ground beside the Gandaka river a week ago and promptly informed his master. The Brahmin instructed him to inform the Chief Eunuch, the guardian of the harem, without revealing his identity. A message was thrust into the eunuch's hand as he wound his way through the crowded bazar on his way to his favourite opium den. He promptly set aside all thoughts of heavenly oblivion and rushed off to see the girl's body. His man followed. The spymaster had expected the eunuch to inform Ashoka immediately. He hadn't. Instead, he had tried to cover up the murder, fearing royal wrath.

The Brahmin had watched his movements for a week, surprised and increasingly alarmed. He had never suspected that the eunuch was on familiar terms with so many powerful men in the kingdom – noblemen, court officials, spies working under diplomatic cover and, most surprising of all, the prime minister Radhagupta himself. How had he missed it, he thought, his mouth drawn in a grim line. His spies at court and in the harem had much to answer for.

When the Brahmin brought the news to the king, Ashoka flew into a rage and summoned the Chief Eunuch. Under the king's questioning, the eunuch was too terrified to speak coherently. The king immediately dispatched him to prison, where he would be tortured for information. He also ordered that Radhagupta would oversee the interrogation. Ashoka's wrath was terrible to watch.

'She was killed seven days ago? And this fool doesn't even tell me? And you…' Ashoka glared at the Brahmin, quite indifferent to the screams of the eunuch, who was being dragged away by the guards.

'Perhaps he was scared, Your Majesty,' the Brahmin answered with a straight face.

'When did you get to know of the murder?'

'Just seven days ago, Your Majesty. But I was watching the Chief Eunuch, hoping he would lead me to the killer.'

'Obviously he didn't,' the king said drily. 'Except for following the damned fellow around, what else have your spies discovered?'

When the Brahmin told him, the king's jaw dropped in surprise.

'You found her in a cremation ground? One of my harem girls? What was she doing there?'

'My spies are investigating, sire. Her body had been flung on a half-burned pyre and was partially charred. Her face was gone. We also found a pair of black cestus lying a few feet away from the body, hidden under a pile of firewood.'

'What the hell is a cestus?'

'It's a glove made of leather straps, used by Greek fighters. Some ladies of the court of Philip of Macedon decided to stylise it. They made fine silk versions and introduced them in court as high fashion. I believe Olympias, Alexander's mother, started the trend, but it didn't quite catch on.' He paused, then continued, 'Queen Asandhimitra wears them sometimes.'

Asandhimitra was the queen of Magadha.

'The queen can do what she likes. But why was my concubine wearing Greek gloves? If her face was destroyed by fire, how could you tell she was one of mine?'

'My spy came to know the Chief Eunuch had identified her by a crescent-shaped birthmark on her hand. Blood had congealed in her back, indicating that she had been killed and then burnt.'

'Go on.'

'There were no signs of a struggle, indicating that she knew the killer. She wasn't kidnapped either, or my agents would have heard of it.'

It wasn't easy for an outsider to get into Ashoka's harem, or any other part of the palace where the women lived. Male and female attendants constantly watched over them. Neither the king nor Queen Asandhimitra knew that some of these watchers were the Brahmin's agents.

'Aren't you and your people supposed to keep track of the goings on in my palace, especially in my harem?' Ashoka swore and flung his wine pot to the ground. The burnished clay shattered into pieces and wine splattered on the Brahmin's feet. He did not react.

'Find the killer and bring his head to me, Brahmin. For seven days, you kept this murder a secret from me. Now, you have seven days to solve it, or it will be your sacred skin in Chandagirika's hands,' Ashoka warned.

Chandagirika, Girika for short, was Ashoka's feared chief torturer. He practised his macabre craft in the infamous prison of Pataliputra, named Narak Vatika, the Palace of Hell. It was a large building, one of the most beautiful in the city. Inside, however, existed the most hellish prison and torture chamber in the kingdom.

So few days to solve a week-old murder?

The Brahmin couldn't believe that the king would carry out his threat. If Ashoka trusted anyone at all, it was him. A little.

The truth was that the king was as capable of trust as a horse of flying. He had captured the throne by murdering his brother Sushima, who had been tricked to death by Magadha's wily prime minister Radhagupta, who then went on to serve Ashoka. Radhagupta had an uncanny knack for survival.

The Brahmin knew the prime minister hated him; hated his independence and refusal to bow to him; hated how close he was to the king.

It was a hot day and Ashoka's coarse, dark skin was covered with a fine sheen of sweat. It was common knowledge that the king was sensitive when it came to his appearance. He had once put to death all the women in his harem after he had overheard one of them complain that she couldn't bear to touch his pox-marked body. However, the murder of his concubine had hurt his pride.

'Who else knows of the murder?' Ashoka asked grimly.

The Brahmin paused. The moment had come. Palace politics had to be played with the delicacy of a game of chess, and followed up with the blunt force of a mace. He said, 'The Chief Eunuch first went to the prime minister, sire.'

'You mean, Radhagupta knew?' The king's eyes narrowed.

'It would appear so, Your Majesty,' the Brahmin answered. 'I thought he had informed you.'

The king bared his teeth in a mockery of a smile. In its cruelty and power, the Brahmin saw why the people of Magadha had named him the Black Prince when he was just a commander in the army of his father, Bindusara.

'You hate Radhagupta, don't you?' Ashoka asked.

'As he hates me,' the Brahmin replied.

The king nodded. 'A prime minister cannot keep secrets from his king. Nor can a spymaster.'

Suddenly his voice changed.

'Does the queen know of the murder too?' he snapped.

'No, Your Majesty. She is preparing to leave for Ujjain. She is bored here. She says the war has become your mistress.'

'I suppose she told you that herself?' Ashoka asked darkly. He knew that Asandhimitra liked and trusted the Brahmin. 'She hasn't told *me* yet that she is leaving for Ujjain.'

The Brahmin cleared his throat. It was a delicate situation.

'You aren't married, are you, spymaster?'

'I am wedded to Magadha.'

'Good answer, though such an explanation from me would not satisfy my queen.'

The Brahmin wondered why Ashoka should suddenly choose to share such a personal detail with him. But then, the king was as unpredictable as a thunderstorm in summer. The Brahmin chose his words carefully.

'My lord, you have been busy conferring with your generals. The queen knows that,' he said.

Two deep creases appeared on the king's forehead. He stroked his rough, black beard.

'If even a hair on her head is threatened, I promise Girika will flay you alive and throw you to the vultures.'

Now that was a promise Ashoka would keep.

'Her Majesty is safe, my lord. She is going to Ujjain under armed escort. I've chosen the guards myself.'

The king's eyes took on a dreamy expression. 'Ah, lucky her. I love Ujjain, though I only keep a small harem there,' he said.

A small harem of about eight hundred young women, the Brahmin thought with amusement. And, like all harems, claustrophobic with deceit, jealousy and petty power play. The queen would spend most of her time pacifying her husband's restless concubines – some of whom he would never even meet.

'I'm considering going to Ujjain too. Her Majesty may be able to help me catch the killer,' the spymaster said, choosing his words carefully.

Ashoka glared at the Brahmin. 'What does she have to do with the murder?'

'Since it is the queen who selects the king's concubines from the Chamber of the Virgins, she may remember something about the murdered girl.'

The Chamber of the Virgins had been built by King Bindusara in the north of Pataliputra, on the banks of the Gandaka. Beautiful young women were brought there for the king's pleasure. Asandhimitra chose the girls she believed her husband would like best from among them and despatched them to Ashoka's various harems in Ujjain, Taxila, Suvarnagiri and Kausambi.

'How dare you assume the queen knows something about the murder?' Ashoka growled.

The Brahmin ignored the royal interruption and

continued, 'The cestus … she may know which of the ladies wear them.'

Court fashion was as much about sycophancy and imitation as it was about style and ostentation.

Ashoka grunted dismissively, though the Brahmin sensed that the mystery perplexed him. He knew the king needed him to be more vigilant now than at any other time. Ashoka was preparing for war with Kalinga, a powerful kingdom to Magadha's east, and Pataliputra was teeming with spies who crowded the taverns, brothels and inns patronized by common soldiers and noblemen alike. In a display of rare intuition Ashoka asked, 'So what have your spies learned so far from frequenting the filthy taverns? Or are they spending my silver from the royal coffers just for the fun of it? I have a good mind to throw the whole sorry lot of you in jail.'

'That would hardly help, Your Majesty. A good cup of soma or a tumble in the bed of a young whore gives up more secrets than Girika can elicit from his Palace of Hell.'

Ashoka looked doubtful. He was aware that the Brahmin disliked the use of torture. The spymaster believed it was possible to inflict more pain on the mind than on the body.

Girika, on the other hand, revelled in inflicting pain. Especially on the travelling monks from the northern kingdom of Kapilavastu, who preached the gospel of the Buddha. They never begged for mercy, nor uttered a word, seemingly impervious to pain even while they were being tortured. This wounded his professional pride.

Ashoka, at the instance of Radhagupta and the powerful brahmins of his court, who considered the Buddha's egalitarian teachings a danger to their influence, had ordered his soldiers to arrest all such monks who entered the city and hand them over to Girika, who spread-eagled them on red-hot iron sheets and poured molten metal down their throats and branded their faces with hot irons.

Ironically, it was one such monk who had inspired him to invent such ingenious and horrific torture techniques. His demeanour had annoyed Girika the moment the guards brought him into the torture chamber. He had greeted Girika with a serene smile, as if the thought of the agony that awaited him was amusing. 'Pain is an illusion that tests man's courage,' he said as the guards manacled his feet and tightened the iron cuffs around his wrists.

When Girika interrogated him, all he would speak of was a new prophet who walked in the Buddha's footsteps and freed men from the pain of karma by showing them the true path of courage.

This interested the torturer. The Buddha's teachings challenged the pre-eminence of the upper castes in the land. Now, a new messiah who propagated the same views in Magadha? Radhagupta would pay well for this piece of news.

When Girika pressed for more information, the monk replied that only a man of true knowledge could recognize the new prophet. Those without such knowledge were condemned to the prison of ignorance, where they would experience the five tortures of hell. There, demons would fling prisoners down on a burning iron floor and iron stakes would be driven through their hands, feet and heart.

Girika, to Ashoka's great delight, decided to adopt these sadistic methods, reserving them for special prisoners. He also innovated. Ashoka loved to watch his chief torturer chop Buddhist monks into octagonal shapes, then hexagons, squares, ovals and finally circles with his red-hot axe. But he was always surprised at the stoicism with which they bore the torment. 'It's a pity these idiots aren't soldiers,' he would say wistfully. 'They can withstand so much pain.'

The king rose from his seat now, tightly gripping the Brahmin's shoulder with his huge hand. The Brahmin knew he was looking for any sign of pain and decided to deny him the pleasure. Unaware of his spymaster's thoughts, Ashoka said, 'Your spies are bringing me good information. With our increased war taxes, our troops are better paid, and have good weapons and fresh horses. But a murder in the palace is a serious matter. If someone can get into my harem and kill my women, they can get me too.'

A sharika bird cried out, the shrill sound of warning.

'Have my enemies slipped a snake into my garden now?' Ashoka demanded. Sharikas were highly prized for their ability to sense the approach of snakes.

The Brahmin permitted himself a smile. 'Even if they did, the gardeners would have killed it,' he replied.

'Yes, true killers, my gardeners,' the king muttered sarcastically. The Brahmin pretended not to have heard.

A breeze waltzed browning leaves down to the grass, followed by a shower of jasmine flowers.

Ashoka followed their path with his eyes. 'My girls always smell of jasmine,' he said quietly, as though speaking to himself.

He bent suddenly, scooped up a fistful of fallen flowers and flung them at the Brahmin's face.

'Find the murderer, Brahmin, find him and bring him to me,' he said in sudden rage, bringing his face close to his spymaster's. 'Seven days are all you get.'

The Brahmin didn't flinch. But behind his expressionless face his mind was churning faster than the wheels of a Magadhan war chariot. Ashoka's deadline meant the invasion was to start soon.

The king returned to his seat and watched his spy chief keenly for a long moment. Then he gestured, indicating that the audience was over.

The Brahmin didn't budge. Ashoka's eyebrows rose.

'There is something more about the girl's murder, sire, more disturbing than the murder itself. A red flower was found inside the cestus. A kovidara. A blood flower.'

Ashoka's cheek muscles twitched. 'A blood flower? Do you think this is the work of that assassin who is known to leave a kovidara beside the body of his victims?' he asked.

The Brahmin looked thoughtful. He didn't answer.

Ashoka continued, 'The Kalingans must have sent the Blood Flower to kill me, no doubt. The sneaky bastards don't want to face me on the battlefield. Did you know that their ambassador, that sneaky Lord Suma has asked for an audience? Well, I'll let the representative of the Kalinga court know that Ashoka isn't frightened of assassins, however famous they may be.'

The Brahmin hadn't heard of the ambassador's request. He was now really angry with his informants in the palace; someone was going to pay for this carelessness. However, his expression gave away nothing. The king raised a questioning eyebrow. 'I do not doubt Your Majesty's courage,' the Brahmin responded. 'But if the Blood Flower is in Pataliputra, we must be careful,' the Brahmin warned. 'I've already assigned the case to my best agent. I've tripled the guard around the royal chambers, sire, and added more Greek fighters to the king's guard. They will accompany you everywhere, all the time.'

'And also put more archers on the watchtowers, I noticed. But I'm not as easy to kill as a poor young girl from my harem.' Ashoka glanced at his spymaster briefly. The Brahmin was the only man, besides himself, who was allowed into the harem. Such was his trust in him.

'Remember, the Blood Flower shouldn't get anywhere near the queen,' Ashoka warned, the threat explicit in his voice.

'I give you my word, sire. I'll die defending the queen.'

'That wouldn't help me or her,' Ashoka barked. 'Now go. You have a murderer to catch and an assassin to stop. I hope you can do it in seven days.'

The Brahmin missed the look of malice Ashoka threw in his direction as he left. But it was not missed by Radhagupta, who walked in just then with a sheaf of parchments under his arm. He gave the Brahmin a cold nod, which was acknowledged with a faint smile. One of the reasons Radhagupta hated the Brahmin was that the spymaster was allowed to turn his back on the king, a privilege only close family members were allowed. He had raised the matter once and Ashoka had replied, 'Even with his back turned, the man knows what I am thinking.'

Radhagupta had not bothered to conceal his disbelief.

As the Brahmin walked towards the garden gate, which led into the palace grounds, he heard Ashoka's hearty welcome of his prime minister and sensed the thunderstorm behind the joviality. He decided to stop behind the gate and watch.

Ashoka threw a muscular arm around Radhagupta's shoulder. 'We go to war soon, and the army is in the final phases of training,' the king's voice boomed. 'It's a war I don't intend to lose. I hope your good-for-nothings in the administration are ready to run whatever is left of Kalinga's affairs once I'm finished with it.' The Brahmin could hear Radhagupta's acquiescing murmur.

'By the way, my learned prime minister, do you know anything about a dead concubine?' Ashoka asked in a deceptively mild voice. The Brahmin smiled to himself. This did not bode well for Radhagupta.

A Fatal Secret

7600 BC
Lanka

'You want her back so desperately that you can't eat or sleep,' the great king of Lanka spat the words at the man who had come to kill him. 'Try and take her if you can.'

Divisions of infantry, cavalry and chariots covered the great, sandy battlefield by the sea. The ascetic prince of Ayodhya, whose wife had been abducted by the Lankan king, scowled.

'I will,' he said through clenched teeth. 'And I will take your life too.'

The king smiled slyly. 'It's not just her that you want,' he taunted. 'You want something more. Something of mine that could make you the most powerful man on earth.'

The prince gave a triumphant laugh and said, 'Oh yes, and it will. I hear the Golden Scythe can mow down armies and cities in the blink of an eye. When this battle is over, and you lie dead at my feet, I will take away both my wife and your weapon. With it, I will rain the fires of hell down on my enemies. No one in the world will dare stand against me then.'

The Golden Scythe. The deadly, shining little cone, the ultimate thunderbolt of destruction, the gold-tipped missile that contained the power to bring about the end of the world. Its legend had spread far and wide across the known world, and many invaders, adventurers and spies had tried to steal it. None succeeded, and most died at the hands of the king's torturers and executioners.

The king knew there was nothing more powerful than a legend to make a ruler invincible. The legend of the Golden Scythe was the most terrifying legend of all. It was created in the king's vast subterranean laboratory complex in a faraway mountain forest, guarded night and day by thousands of heavily armed and specially armoured soldiers. Here, his best scientists worked on building weapons and conducting experiments with new and strange substances that sailors brought from all over the world. The Golden Scythe was their crowning glory.

It began like this. One day, a ship arrived from the western lands, full of dying seamen. It also bore a cargo of a heavy black mineral, which a dying sailor reported had been discovered in silver mines in a cold country far away. They had learned of its power, which caused slow death to anyone who touched it or even went near it. It caused blindness and the skin to blister, he said, until the victims died screaming in agony, bleeding from every pore. After the infected sailors had been cremated on the sea shore itself, the deadly cargo was brought in iron boxes to the king's forest laboratory. The bearers died in agony a few days later and the king was impressed by the terrible and invisible power of this substance, which could kill from a distance in spite of being encased in iron.

Being a great scholar himself, the king knew that it

was written in the scriptures and the teachings of sages that god lived in the core of everything in the universe. He was the power in every seed, invisible and coiled up like the great serpent Ananta, until he exploded as a primeval force, creating forests on desert lands and floods that wiped out nations. The king instructed his scientists to find the ore's power source. They tried for months and many died in the process, for exposure meant slow, agonising death. Until one scientist had an epiphany that there must be some unknown substance in the silver mines that contained the foreign mineral's malefic influence. Lead was the answer.

Giant rooms lined with lead were built, inside which they worked for years, breaking the deadly substance into minute pieces, which were then exposed to various forces in an attempt to discover the core. And find it they did, at great cost, when one day a great explosion happened; a fire of deathly power, reducing the laboratory and large areas around it into a wasteland. Forest dwellers, soldiers, the guards, all other living things and the scientists themselves were wiped out by its force. Whole villages nearby were incinerated. From the explosion rose a gigantic mushroom cloud that tore asunder the skies, which vomited red rain for days, burning the land and all living things on it. Rivers, streams and lakes boiled over, killing all the fish and underwater creatures. Children were born deformed in villages and hamlets, which had escaped the intensity of the explosion but were still close by. They took sick and died soon thereafter. No bird or animal would venture into that great circle of destruction.

Having realised the power of the strange ore, the chief scientist at the king's court and his team fashioned a cone-shaped weapon to contain it. They then built a trigger for it, which only the king could operate. It was christened the Golden Scythe, because of the dazzling glow of its explosion and the sweeping deathwind that followed in expanding circles of destruction.

Going by previous experience, they also knew that the Scythe poisoned anyone who touched it. The scientists added lead to glass in a heated furnace using sea-coal, creating a new element to control the cone's power – lead glass. The Scythe was encased in it.

Knowing the power of the weapon, the king wisely ordered his scientists to create a counter weapon. An item had to be found that could neutralize its effects. Emissaries travelled far and wide, meeting wise men and charlatans alike, searching for such a matter. One day, a hermit arrived in the capital from the Himalayas with a seed which he claimed had the power to heal broken things – both animate and inanimate. He called it the mrita sanjeevani. The royal scientists conducted experiments on the seed, which grew on the faraway Dunagiri mountain above a valley of flowers. When they discovered its core after many attempts, it bloomed in the shape of a cloud of silver light, which revived the devastated forest and cured those afflicted by its twin.

Recalling these incidents of long ago on the battlefield of the present, the king felt sad that the Lord of Ayodhya, blinded by vengeance, did not realise there was more to the Golden Scythe than destruction and despair. Nothing in the Universe existed without balance. Not even the Scythe. Anger and bitterness welled up in him at the futility of it all.

'Let's end this,' he bellowed in fury.

His army, men who had lost sons, fathers and brothers, took up his roar. He felt the power of their grief and remembered his own brothers and sons, who had perished on this same bloody mud field one by one. Now only nine of his brothers remained; they had all been born, one after the other, to his father, the great brahmin sage Vishrava, and mother, Princess Kaikesi, in their ashram deep in the forest. They had been raised as a secret band, each one a brother of shadows. Growing up in the forest, they had been taught powerful mantras which gave their minds a supernatural keenness and strengthened their will. They were coached in the subtle arts of espionage and psychological warfare. They were trained in archery, the use of swords and axes, and to bring down fast-moving objects with javelins and spears.

Now they were arrayed behind their brother and king, astride their huge warhorses. They were his nine heads: counsellors of wisdom, strategy, statecraft, astrology, science, duty, love, compassion and secrecy. With these qualities, as one, they were undefeatable. But the tenth head had not sought their counsel when he took the woman. They knew he would pay for his mistake and sorrowed. The king of Lanka felt their sorrow as his own. But being a man of action, he gestured to the nearest one, the eldest of the nine, and pulled out two gold cones encased in glass from holsters on his war belt. His hand flashed. In a single fluid movement his brother caught the cones in mid-air, wheeled his horse around and galloped away into the forest with the others riding hard behind him. They knew the implications. The war would be over soon, but not for them. Other wars would be fought by different kings in distant lands throughout time, and the Scythe and its twin had to be protected from them all.

When the prince of Ayodhya saw the nine brahmin horsemen vanish into the forest, he urged his gigantic chariot forward with an angry cry, which resounded across the battlefield. His screaming legions followed.

It is ending at last, the king of Lanka thought. A mighty wind filled his ears, deafening him. His enemy had released the brahmastra, the most powerful missile in his armoury. Only the Golden Scythe could have countered it, but it was too late for that.

Night descended upon the earth.

In the middle of the spreading darkness, floated the woman he coveted but could never have. She looked as she had on the day he stole her, with lustrous eyes and a deep-red smile; dark hair and skin like moonlight on ivory. He begged her to come into his arms and forgive him, but instead felt a brief moment of great pain, an explosion of fire and ash and then a calm, vast emptiness in which he slowly drifted, dreaming of the fragrant gardens of Ashoka Van.

Thus the great brahmin king of Lanka died.

The Loyal Assassin

Leaving the king and the prime minister in the royal garden, the Brahmin left for the Ministry of Secrets, where he spent the night receiving reports from his spies on the reactions of people in the city and the palace to the Chief Eunuch's arrest. As he set the last report aside – something on the theft of grain from the royal warehouses – and prepared for bed, he was satisfied that the work of his spies had exceeded his expectations though the thought some of his men in the palace had bungled still rankled in his mind. As it is with men who make momentous decisions about the life and death of others, his sleep was short but untroubled. After the morning's ablutions, he started on his rounds, reviewing the security arrangements for the day.

He moved like a ghost through the breaking morning, along the shaded palace verandah, his eyes briefly caught by the iridescent peacock feather fans that rotated on wooden rods overhead. They were connected by long ropes which ran the length of the verandah, looping back into a complex system of waterwheels that kept them turning incessantly. The Brahmin padded along silently, marvelling yet again at the skill of the painters and sculptors who had covered the wooden pillars that supported the slanting, tiled palace roof with tiny figures engaged in hunting, dancing, singing, even making love. He loved the chauris the most: statues of voluptuous women with whisks in their hands – Ashoka's favourite figurines, which he insisted be included in all the friezes in the palace.

The vast complex included the king's dwelling, the mansions of various minor queens and princes, the courts, the ministerial chambers and the armoury. The Brahmin strode past the great stone-paved square with the stables by the eastern wall and next to it, the gigantic sheds that housed five hundred war elephants. Their trumpeting often frightened the visitors who came to see the marvels of Pataliputra from all over the kingdom and sometimes sparked stampedes. Towards the southern corner of the grounds stood the execution block and the large stone platform where traitors were torn apart by wild horses. The jails and dungeons were in the western corner, built with black stone and guarded by huge iron gates affixed to heavy slabs of timber. On either side of the northern entrance, with its soaring towers and great gates, stood the gulmas – the barracks of Ashoka's personal guard.

Away from all these impressive buildings, behind the palace, stood the Ministry of Secrets – an unassuming single-storeyed yellow brick building set in a small leafy enclosure named the Garden of Secrets. It was here he worked and lived, in a low circular building connected to the main palace by a narrow corridor that bisected a large well-tended garden, which he had insisted should be free of flowers of any kind. Instead, there was a large expanse of immaculate green lawns, planted with hedges and old trees. The building's humble exterior belied its impregnable defenses – a reinforced iron door designed to resist the most powerful battering ram, thick stone walls strong enough to withstand any assault. Here the Brahmin spent much of his time, unravelling or weaving conspiracies, running a vast espionage network that stretched from the borders of Greece and Persia to China, Viet Land and Lanka. His informants thrived in the households of nobles and merchants, all the ranks in the Magadha army and all the forts in the kingdom, the convivial chambers of the city's brothels and the secluded rooms and halls of the harem. They were called gudhapurushas and were organised in two divisions – sansthana purushas and sanchari purushas. The first, who infiltrated households and offices, were watchers and informers while the second travelled the length and breadth of the kingdom, gathering intelligence. This system, devised by Chanakya, Chandragupta's great general of the mind, and laid out in the *Arthasastra*, was so effective that it had remained unchanged by three generations of Magadhan rulers. It was now the Brahmin's turn to preside over the gigantic enterprise.

People from all over the kingdom thronged the palace grounds daily in great numbers. They arrived in Pataliputra with a mercy plea for an imprisoned family member or a request for restitution subsequent to official maltreatment or an audience with the king, begging his favour for a commercial enterprise. Some sought employment in the palace complex as artisans, carpenters, masons, sculptors, cooks or messenger boys. Others came just to gawk. Amidst the crowds operated any number of pickpockets and tricksters, trying to sell everything, including the river Indus, to gullible merchants from the provinces. There were pimps, petty criminals and gangs of robbers disguised as peasants, some of them with shining, oiled weapons concealed under dirty shawls, ready to attack the oxcarts which brought gold to the treasury. Most of them ended up as food for the crocodiles in the palace moat. The guards who apprehended them believed in meting out swift justice.

Observing the day's visitors, the Brahmin thought how easy it would be for an assassin to hide amidst the teeming multitude. A gaggle of urchins stood around a fire-eating juggler and his monkey. As if sensing his scrutiny, one of them turned and gave a small, impudent smile before turning back to the juggler. The spymaster sighed at the cheekiness of his little spy. He looked around the complex and a frown puckered his forehead briefly.

There must be around twenty thousand people here, he thought, and about a hundred of them were his spies. But there could never be enough. His men had spent the days and nights following the discovery of the concubine's body and the kovidara beside it, searching for signs of intruders or anything out of the ordinary in the palace grounds. But the killer or killers had vanished like wraiths in the mist that trawled the surface of the Gandaka river at dawn, leaving echoes of distant, ominous whispers.

'I heard you,' he barked without turning around.

'So demoralizing,' said the woman who had materialized by his side. 'I'm supposed to be the best of your spies, but why is it that I can't ever surprise you?'

If only you knew how much you do surprise me, Hao Tran, my beautiful assassin, my ivory-skinned weapon of seduction and murder and the one I trust the most – were such a thing possible.

'You are indeed the best, Hao, but perhaps my hearing is very keen today,' he said kindly.

He felt her breath, scented with spices and pomegranate seeds, on the side of his neck. Swiftly he gathered his thoughts and said, 'I told the king I had sent my best agent to investigate the concubine's murder. What have you found?'

'Nothing much, except rumours that the Blood Flower is here to kill Ashoka,' she answered. The Brahmin smiled; she never called him king.

'Sent by Nandidevi, I bet,' he said thoughtfully.

General Nandidevi was the commander of the armies of Srutayush, the boy-king of Kalinga. Hao and her master had foiled several previous attempts on Ashoka's life. Some of the assassins had died trying while others confessed under torture that they had been hired by the Kalingan general. The Brahmin had heard the Blood Flower was known to never fail. Neither was he.

However, the grim specter of failure was not far from his thoughts. In the world of lies, doubt was a constant companion and truth was just a corpse in an alleyway. He had to defeat the general and his pet assassin at any cost, or else the king and the kingdom he had sworn to protect would be destroyed.

Sensing his mood, Hao touched his shoulder briefly. The Brahmin smiled down at her.

Hao was around five feet and three inches tall, with a slim, taut body. She wore a white cotton blouse and fitted brown silk pantaloons. Her thick, black hair was piled high on her head and held in place by a tiny ivory comb. Her body could be an instrument of murder or love, but it was her face the Brahmin found most arresting: the triangular jawline, the slanting eyes of her race, dark and challenging under arched brows. He had often wondered what it would feel like to draw her closer by her waist, feel her against his warrior's body and crush her lips with his. But he never allowed his eyes to betray his thoughts, for he was master of them all, even her.

It was three years now since he had rescued Hao from execution, after she had killed a man at the slave brothel she had been sold into. Her victim was a junior court official, who had wanted to cut her up for fun. Instead, she had grabbed his knife and slit his throat. Something in her face as she passed him on the way to the execution ground, dragged by two laughing guards, had caused the Brahmin to stop. It was a face that refused to be defeated even when confronted by certain death.

Looking at Hao beside him now, the spymaster knew he could expect no gratitude for his act of kindness. She was a child of fate, capable of unflinching loyalty towards the man who had rescued her from certain death. But she never displayed any emotions. She had met his eyes on that day which was to have been her last among the living, and had recognized a cold sympathy in them and had known instantly her life was safe.

'Do you really think there is a connection between the concubine and the Blood Flower because the kovidara was found in the cremation ground?' she asked the Brahmin. 'In this business, one can never be sure of anything.'

The spymaster recalled the deadly floral calling card. So trite. So vain. However good you were at the killing game, vanity was a fatal flaw.

'Why don't you find out?' he asked.

'I can do that by visiting the Chief Eunuch in prison. He was the dead girl's guardian. But I don't think Chandagirika will approve.'

The Brahmin grinned.

'You don't have to go as far as the Palace of Hell to meet the eunuch.'

Hao nodded as he gave her detailed instructions, then slipped away as silently as she had come, a ghost in a palace of shadows. The Brahmin walked on, watching for the unseen and expecting the unexpected.

Mission of Fear

He loved the warm feel of the winter sun on his face. It was getting to be afternoon and the day was bright and clear. Sunlight glowed upon the burnished wooden walls of the main building in the centre of the palace complex. Ashoka had fortified his capital even better than his predecessors, with a great timber palisade and an outer city wall of stone encircled by a deep moat. The massive city gates were made of heavy timber, banded with iron and protected by huge, cruel spikes. Tall guard towers on the first wall afforded an unobstructed view of the outlying plains and the forest beyond. Arrow slits interrupted its entire length. Only a fool would dare attack Ashoka's capital, as Hao had once commented wryly to the Brahmin.

As he strode swiftly through the palace complex, crossing open squares and stepping in and out of a maze of corridors, he smelt war in the air. He glanced up at the five hundred and seventy guard towers that topped the soaring, crenelated city wall at regular intervals, from which vigilant soldiers looked out for signs of hostile action. The forest itself, with its narrow ravines and slippery paths, was a line of defence against any enemy unwise enough to attack Pataliputra.

Sunlight washed the paved stones of the wide street that ran the length of the palisade. The Brahmin knew it was incredibly difficult to scale the city wall, or even to enter Pataliputra unseen through any of the sixty-four gates protected by portcullises and soldiers – but not impossible. In his shadowy world, the spymaster knew that death was a persistent hunter.

'How did the Blood Flower get in, if at all the Blood Flower did?' the Brahmin mused.

Having reached the inner palace, he walked up the flight of steps to the wide verandah that encircled the building. In perfect symmetry, along the verandahs lined with polished Chunar sandstone, stood high teak doors that led inside to various parts of the building. Greek mercenaries wearing leather helmets, tunics, skirts and sandals guarded every door. Each soldier was armed with a xiphos, a short, leaf-shaped sword, and a huge iron-tipped spear. Alexander's men had used these effectively to subdue the war elephants of Porus in the battle of Hydaspes on the banks of the Jhelum river. After Porus's defeat, the fighting skills of the Greek warriors had become known throughout Magadha and beyond. Ashoka's grandfather, Chandragupta, had hired them in his wars against the Nanda kings, whom he deposed to become the ruler of Magadha. He had regarded the Greeks as his best fighters. So did Bindusara. The Brahmin knew that Ashoka, influenced by his grandfather, also had a special fondness for his Greek soldiers, whom he even employed as palace guards.

However, unknown to the king, the Brahmin had recruited some of them as his agents. One of the guards met the Brahmin's eye. The spymaster gave an imperceptible nod and walked through a doorway. It led to a small hall, which widened out into a large room with wooden walls. Here, he waited for his spy.

'Antochlius, there is little time to lose,' he said when the Greek entered. 'Is the dancing girl ready?'

'She is, my lord.'

'Does she know what is expected of her?'

The guard nodded nervously. The things he had heard about the Brahmin terrified him. The Brahmin terrified everyone.

'Does she look like the girl you brought to me two weeks ago?'

Antochlius nodded again, recalling the form and features of the girl his master was referring to and the circumstances in which he had discovered her existence. Two weeks before the concubine's murder, an informer of his, a eunuch who owed him a favour, had told him that one of the harem girls had met the Chief Eunuch in private. She was apparently a new arrival to the harem, but he couldn't identify her, since guards, however trusted, were not allowed inside the women's quarters.

The following day, as he walked to his post, a strange girl had stepped out from behind a pillar, where she had been hiding. Antochlius instinctively grabbed the hilt of his xiphos, but she arrested him with a hand on his forearm.

'Don't. I mean no harm. I want to meet your master,' she had said in a low, cultured voice. He couldn't place her accent, though she spoke Magadha Prakrit perfectly.

'My master?'

'Don't pretend to be stupid. I know you are one of the Brahmin's men.'

'Who told you?'

'A little bird in the harem, who do you think?'

'Where did you come from, my lady?' he had asked, the salutation coming naturally. Something in her face told him here was a woman, however young, who was used to command.

'I have a message for the Brahmin. Take me to him. But I don't want anyone to know.'

The imperiousness in her voice left him no choice but to obey. Yet, he hesitated.

'Why should I? I don't know you,' he began.

The expression in the girl's eyes had stopped him. It held both anger and fear in equal measure.

He knew intuitively then, that this was the girl his informer had spoken about; the girl who had met the Chief Eunuch in private. If she was not, taking her to meet the Brahmin was as good an idea as falling into a cauldron of boiling oil in Girika's chamber. But if she was, the master would be pleased and a promotion might be possible.

Something in the girl's carriage made him decide in her favour.

'Take me to him, soldier,' she repeated. 'But beware, no one should know. Especially the Chief Eunuch.'

If Antochlius had any hesitation in taking this young stranger to the Brahmin, her last statement decided it for him. He had asked her to wait for night to fall so that he could take her to the Brahmin safely. It was the right decision, for the spymaster had greeted her courteously at the gated entrance of the long, covered aisle, which led into his office. To Antochlius's disappointment, he had been asked to wait at the door through the brief meeting and couldn't hear a word of their conversation. Soon the Brahmin came out with the girl, and bid her goodbye with a bow. Antochlius was mystified. She must be someone important for his master to treat her with such respect.

'Until we meet in Ujjain, then,' he heard the Brahmin say.

The girl smiled and left the building swiftly, keeping to the shadowy sheltered side of the corridor with Antochlius behind her. Upon reaching the door of the harem, she turned around and glanced at him briefly. He read both gratitude and relief in her eyes and felt inexplicably vindicated.

She met him again the next day, creeping up on him as he stood with his back to the doorway, spear gripped firmly in hand. He turned at her touch, and started when he saw it was her. A reproach came to his lips, which he stopped in mid-sentence. There was not one girl who stood beside him now, but two. Seeing his baffled expression, they laughed.

Then they both held out their hands. There were two identical birthmarks on them. The puzzled guard had searched their faces, and found one pair of eyes that was unmistakeable. They belonged to a person who was used to having her orders obeyed.

'Isn't she lovely?' she had asked laughing, pointing to her lookalike. 'I found her in the harem.'

They bore an eerie resemblance to each other, his

new acquaintance and the concubine. A concubine who would be dead two weeks later.

Now, facing his master, Antochlius hoped the Brahmin had not missed the significance of the resemblance. Obviously he hadn't. He had ordered Antochlius to find a girl who looked like her, and be ready to leave at a moment's notice. He guessed the time had come.

As if he sensed Antochlius's thoughts, the Brahmin clapped him on the shoulder and said curtly. 'Take the dancing girl, wherever you have hidden her, to my office. The girl you brought to me will already be there. Let them get acquainted. Two hours after the moon has set, bring them to the pavilion behind the Ministry of Secrets for final instructions. Keep the horses saddled and ready to leave at my signal. You will be met by a contingent of mounted guards outside the palace gate, who will take you to the queen's palace in Ujjain. You understand the need for secrecy? I will follow you later.'

'There is a complication, master,' Antochlius said hesitantly. The Brahmin frowned. He did not like complications. They meant death in his trade.

'The girl wants to bring someone along with her,' the Greek said. 'An older woman.'

The Brahmin didn't like it.

'Who is she?' he asked tersely.

'I didn't recognize her, sir. She was heavily veiled and was wearing black gloves when the girl brought her to meet me, but I am certain she is highborn. Maybe she is a minor queen or the lady of some aristocratic house. She has taken a liking to the girl, who seems to trust her and will not leave the palace without her. Maybe she is the one who first told her about me.'

A mysterious lady who had taken a liking to a girl whose life was in danger? She could be a danger herself to the girl. What a mess! The Brahmin looked at his young spy keenly. He was certain Antochlius was hiding something. But the Greek, instead of looking away, met the Brahmin's searching gaze without flinching. It made the Brahmin even more certain that he was not being told the whole story. He swore under his breath.

A black glove had been found near the concubine's corpse. Could this strange woman lead him to the killer?

Or was she the killer?

Keeping her close would force her to reveal her hand, gloves or no gloves. He was confident the guards were competent enough to keep the girl from harm. He resolved to brief them, put them on alert.

He looked sharply at Antochlius.

'Keep a close watch on the woman,' he ordered. 'And when you reach the main crossroads, take the forest path with the girl. That should confuse her new guardian. I will meet on the way.'

Antochlius nodded obediently.

'And be on guard. No harm should befall the girl. Or else I will find you, in whichever snake's burrow you have chosen to crawl into, and make you wish you had never grown up to suck your mother's teat.'

The Greek saw the cruel promise in his master's dark eyes and almost stumbled. 'I'm trusting you with a great secret,' the Brahmin continued. 'And I believe you will carry your mission through.'

The alternative was too terrifying for Antochlius to contemplate.

'And mind you, none of the women should land up on a pyre,' the Brahmin added ominously.

Antochlius sucked in his breath. It was he who had discovered the body of the concubine following an alert from an informer at the cremation ground. Most of the charnel-house keepers and low-caste priests were the Brahmin's secret agents, tasked with recording any mysterious or hasty disposal of bodies. The informer had been drunk at the time of the girl's murder and had not seen the killer.

The Greek suppressed a grin at the memory of the Chief Eunuch's fat form waddling away in a flap to the cremation ground after receiving his message in the bazaar. Observing his man's mirth, the spymaster frowned. The smile vanished.

The Brahmin nodded curtly and walked on, leaving Antochlius to prepare for the long journey to Ujjain.

The scent of sandalwood and flowers lingered in the passageways. Ashoka had rebuilt parts of the palace, including his throne room, the armoury and the treasury, replacing the wooden structures made by his grandfather's master builders with stone. His own quarters and the queen's, as well as of the royal offspring and the harem, remained untouched because the inside walls were made of sandalwood from the deep southern forests. Their fragrance soothed the king as he slept, aroused him when he made love and calmed him when he was in one of his spectacular rages.

The walls inside the palace were draped with rich tapestries that depicted Chandragupta's arrival in Pataliputra and his conquest of Ujjain. Some illustrated the war between Alexander and various kings. Others had richly coloured pictorial descriptions of Chandragupta's conquest of Kashmir and of him crossing the Vindhyas to subdue the Deccan rulers. Not surprisingly, there were no reminders of Bindusara, Ashoka's immediate predecessor, who came after Chandragupta.

Ashoka was born of a brahmin woman who had been forced to serve as Bindusara's barber. Bindusara was so mesmerized by her beauty that he had married her against the wishes of his queens. She bore him a boy whom she named Ashoka, one without sorrow. But the child's skin, from birth, was so coarse and repulsive that Bindusara loathed the sight of him. In the end, this did not stop Ashoka from ascending the Magadhan throne.

Like his grandfather, Ashoka too was a child of destiny, the Brahmin mused. When he was barely out of his teens, the citizens of Ujjain had rebelled against the king. Spotting an opportunity to get rid of his son, Bindusara had sent Ashoka to subdue the rebellion at the head of an army without weapons. Miraculously, Ujjain had greeted Ashoka as a victor and Bindusara had no option but to appoint him viceroy. The inhabitants of the city had handed over all the rebels to Ashoka, who promptly put them to the sword. It was while living in Ujjain for the next few years, that Ashoka had plotted his father's downfall and the death of the crown prince and his ninety-nine half-brothers.

The king had come a long way, but his journey was far from over, the Brahmin reflected, thinking of the war that lay ahead and the weapon that could decide its outcome. A weapon that had the power to destroy the world, not only Kalinga. A weapon he had but recently heard was in Pataliputra. He had to act soon, he knew. There was no time to waste.

Steeped in thought, the Brahmin left for the Ministry of Secrets, the place from where he daily sent out orders that could mean the death of a treasonous but unsuspecting noble in some faraway province or the freedom of an innocent prisoner in one of the royal dungeons. Today, in between the routine work, he spent time talking to a reluctant visitor, who was kept under strict supervision by loyal officers sworn to secrecy. Soon it would be time to set in motion the first phase of his plan to unmask the concubine's murderer and the Blood Flower. He believed they were connected.

His mind went back to Antochlius and his dangerous mission. For an instant, he felt an unfamiliar touch of doubt. He shrugged it off.

He had made arrangements for the girl to reach Ujjain safely and receive Queen Asandhimitra's protection. She would be safe until he got there. He was confident that the mid-way diversion he had planned would be enough to confuse Nandidevi's spies, in case they were watching. But he also knew that even the best laid plan could be like a fruit sold to unsuspecting villagers in the night market – perfect and shiny on the outside, and hiding a worm at its core.

His thoughts wandered back to Antochlius. What did he know about the girl that he wasn't telling him?

With intuition born out of years of unravelling conspiracies and unmasking secrets, the spymaster guessed it had something to do with the veiled woman.

But it was too late now to change plans.

The trap was set.

Would the killer fall into it?

The City of Hell

Antochlius had been born to a soldier named Aeimnestus of Macedonia, from where Alexander had begun his march to India.

Aeimnestus had started off as a spear-carrier when he was fifteen, like many boys his age in the Greek army. Their job was to clean the soldiers' armour, rub their swords with charcoal and sand until they shone, hone their blades on sharpening stones, wash their clothes and cook for them.

'I would follow Alexander all the way to hell,' Aeimnestus swore to his friends as they sat around a campfire outside the royal tent. Alexander was inside, drinking wine with his lover Hephaestion and a few other companions. 'If only he would make me a soldier.'

As the seemingly invincible Greek army marched through the Achaemenid kingdom, many of its soldiers and generals died. But Aeimnestus's wish came true. After the Greeks stormed Taxila, defeating King Ambhi's armies and slaying him, Aeimnestus was given a sergeant's rank and tasked with guarding a section of the garrison.

When Alexander prepared to leave India at the insistence of the very soldiers who had vowed to follow him to the ends of the earth, Aeimnestus was undecided whether to follow his lord or stay back in Taxila.

'It's too long a walk, through all that wilderness, the deserts and fording rivers,' he said to Sunanda, a slim, doe-eyed girl he had come to know in Taxila.

'You seem to be in a hurry to leave me,' she had said tartly, her dark eyes flashing.

And so Aeimnestus married her and Antochlius was born a year later. Sunanda's father was a soldier who had fought alongside Chandragupta against the Nandas. He got his Macedonian son-in-law a commission in the Magadhan army. The Greek, who was already a battle-hardened man at thirty, fought at his king's side in many wars as Chandragupta – or Sandrocottus, as the Greeks called him – sought to expand his kingdom by the sword. When, at the age of forty-two, Chandragupta abdicated the throne to become a Jain monk, Aeimnestus accompanied him on his long trek to the southern mountains, where he watched his master fast to death on the shores of Shravanabelagola – the White Lake that lay calm and timeless in the middle of a valley.

Before Chandragupta left the palace, his head shaven and clad in a monk's robes, he had made his son, the new king Bindusara, swear that the son of Aeimnestus, when he grew up, would serve in the king's elite bodyguard. Bindusara agreed. By the time Antochlius was of an age to enter military service, Bindusara was dying. The young Greek reminded the king of the promise he had made to his father. True to his word, Bindusara brought Antochlius into the company of the royal bodyguards, where he continued to serve even after the old king died and Ashoka took his place.

One day, while on his way home, Antochlius had been waylaid by a group of thugs. Armed with just a xiphos, he had made short work of them. Instead of informing the captain of the night guard, he had simply tossed their corpses in the moat for the crocodiles to breakfast on; he didn't want the bother of an official enquiry. One of the Brahmin's spotters had learned about the fight and told him about the resourceful young man who had both brains and brawn and could keep secrets. Thus Antochlius ended up joining Magadha's espionage service, where he rapidly rose up the ranks.

Then came the day when he was summoned by the Chief Eunuch.

'I have information that will earn you your master's approval, if not gratitude,' he informed the young Greek.

'My master's gratitude is not earned easily. Besides,what is in it for you? You are the prime minister's lackey,' Antochlius replied, rather recklessly.

'I'm nobody's lackey, my boy, but I have to strike the right balance between your master and Radhagupta to survive in this nest of vipers. Enemies and friends in Pataliputra are as interchangeable as a tavern whore's affections. I am certain my information will earn you a pat on the back from the Brahmin.'

'How so?'

'Tell your master that a Greek soldier was injured in a knife fight at a brothel in Narak Nagari last night and is holed up in an inn there. An ordinary soldier, but with powerful friends.'

'Who is he?'

'Ah, that is for your master to find out. Tell him that discovering the soldier's identity will be to his benefit,' the eunuch replied.

Upon receiving the tip, the Brahmin duly ordered the captain of the guards to check for any soldier who had missed the daily roll call. Some Greek fighters, part of a small group that always stuck together, had not reported for duty the day before. The captain suspected they had deserted and was about to send a mounted contingent to look for them and bring them back to face the music – deserters were flayed alive after their eyes were gouged out and legs chopped off.

Narak Nagari, the City of Hell, had over time spread like an evil canker along the riverbank skirting the edge of the forest. Any stranger who ventured into its warren of narrow, dirty lanes, skirting the piles of donkey dung and offal in the middle of the muddy streets and avoiding the snarling packs of hungry dogs, did so at considerable risk to their person. In Pataliputra, and the numerous other cities and towns of the kingdom, all the streets had water channels leading into the moats, which carried sewage from houses. The punishment for throwing rubbish into them was long spells in prison. But in Narak Nagari, no such rules were followed; the streets overflowed with filth and rats gnawed the corpses of dogs and men to the bone. Most of its denizens were outlaws, murderers, robbers, petty thieves and tricksters – all fleeing Ashoka's justice. There were also the embittered victims of fate – widows who had chosen prostitution over being burnt alive on the pyres of their dead husbands, women who had been cheated of their land and evicted from their homes with nowhere to go, and village girls who had been enticed by procurers and sold to brothel keepers.

Together, Antochlius and the Brahmin set out for this dismal place in search of the wounded Greek. They left behind the well-lit houses of Pataliputra and a few hours later entered the unlit streets of Narak Nagari, reining in their horses frequently to prevent them from slipping in the mud or breaking a leg in some unexpected ditch on the dirty, unpaved road. The sounds of their approach scattered the shadowy figures lurking in the unlit alleys, while others emerged from alleyways, seeking easy prey. The sight of the two armed men astride their great warhorses had them vanishing back into the shadows instantly. Prostitutes stood half hidden in the darkness, their faces gaunt with disease and hunger, beckoning passers-by with exaggeratedly lewd gestures. Behind them, hidden in the darkness, crouched the sickle men, who were known to slit the throat of customers while they fucked the women against walls that stank of spittle and piss.

The Brahmin smelt the rancid odours of rotting meat and decayed vegetables, deep fried in animal fat to disguise their foul taste, emanating from the dimly lit taverns and inns. Their doors were open to the street in welcome to their unsavoury clientele, and inside, men slurped rice beer from terracotta pots and shouted at the serving boys to bring them pig intestines stuffed with minced pork. Large, dirty lanterns suspended from ceilings cast pools of yellow light, distorting the shadows on the floors.

At a sign from Antochlius, the Brahmin drew up Garuda, his great Kamboja stallion, in front of a large two-storeyed inn. Antochlius consulted a rough map the Chief Eunuch had drawn for him and nodded. Garuda whinnied uneasily at the strange smells and raucous laughter from inside the building. Its upper windows were shut, though thin yellow slivers of lamplight showed between the slats. The riders dismounted and looped the reins on the leather saddle horns of their mounts. Antochlius looked worried. He loved his horse. It was his habit to rub down its gleaming coat once every week without fail. Fed on fresh hay and mutton fat mixed with boiled wheat, its powerful muscles stood out.

'Don't worry,' the Brahmin reassured him. 'I wouldn't want to be the stranger who tries to steal Garuda. He is a trained warhorse who loves nothing better than a good fight. So is yours, I presume.'

Antochlius nodded unhappily. The Brahmin patted Garuda's forehead. The great beast gave a soft, pleased whinny. Antochlius observed its deadly steel-tipped hooves, rippling shoulder muscles, large yellow teeth and suppressed a shudder as he followed the Brahmin into the inn. Ruffians sat drinking around rough wooden tables and playing dice. Gaudily painted women, in various stages of undress, sat on the laps of some of the customers. A group of surly looking men was crowded at a corner table, rolling dice and drinking.

A burly bare-chested man with a huge gut spilling over the waistband of his dirty sarong, presumably the inn's landlord, walked up to the visitors. 'You are not welcome here,' he said. 'In fact, we don't like the fancy residents of Pataliputra at all.'

Suddenly a savage neigh, followed by a man's anguished cries, was heard from outside. The cries were abruptly cut short by the repeated thud of blows delivered with great force. All talk and movement ceased inside the inn. Everyone looked towards the door fearfully, as if expecting demons to come charging in. The landlord thrust out his jaw, gesturing to a tall muscular man standing by the door, probably an enforcer, to step out and investigate.

'It's probably my horse, he doesn't like strangers,' the Brahmin drawled, drawing up a stool to sit. Antochlius did likewise.

The enforcer returned, his face ashen, and whispered into the landlord's ear. The landlord rushed out and came back screaming and pulling his hair.

'Your horse just killed a man. It pounded his body into pulp,' he wailed, flailing his arms. The customers had stopped whatever they were doing and were looking at the Brahmin and the weeping landlord. The room clouded darkly with menace. The Brahmin nodded at them pleasantly.

'I told you my horse doesn't like strangers. Especially horse thieves.'

'It's my son-in-law who has been killed,' the landlord shouted, pointing beyond the open door.

'Your daughter married unwisely,' the Brahmin retorted.

A group of men at a table nearby got up, drawing weapons from their belts and from under their shabby garments; sickles, knives and daggers. The women grouped in a corner of the room, their eyes glittering with bloodlust at the prospect of a fight.

'That fine sword by your side isn't going to save you,' someone shouted from the back of the room. 'After we despatch you and your friend, we'll slit your horse's throat and sell its meat to the whores and pimps.'

Later, sitting around the fire drinking with his friends, Antochlius would recall the events that followed. He said he still couldn't figure out exactly what happened. One moment his master was sitting by his side and in the next, with a fluid moment, he had drawn his sword and advanced on the men with a speed that defied the naked eye. He swore he saw him everywhere at once, looming up behind the gamblers, leaping over the tables like an angry tiger and even running upside down on the ceiling. The din of men shouting, women screaming, pots and pans scattering and tables being overturned filled the room. Within moments, it was over. The Brahmin stood by his side, sword lowered, untouched except for a few specks of blood on his shirt and pantaloons. His breathing was even. Most of the inn's patrons lay dead or dying on the floor. Only the landlord stood, frozen in fear, his large protuberant eyes taking in the carnage. The women were screaming and rushing towards the door, each one jostling to be the first out of the room.

'I don't like people threatening my horse,' the Brahmin said cheerfully.

He pushed the landlord gently with his forefinger. The man fell to the ground and then sat up clumsily, his belly resting on his splayed thighs. His face was covered with sweat. His lips trembled. A rat came out from behind a door, sat up on its hind legs, twitching its nose. Another followed and stood beside the first, attracted by the smell of blood.

'Who is upstairs?' the Brahmin asked. 'Or rather, what is upstairs?'

'Nobody,' whispered the landlord. 'There is nothing upstairs.'

'Come, come, don't lie to me. Where is the Greek soldier? Has he become food for the crabs in your filthy canals or dog food in the garbage?'

The man wrung his hands.

'It was a small misunderstanding over dice. One of the players drew his knife but the Greek could look after himself. He finished off three men.'

'Where is he now?'

The landlord licked his lips nervously. Rivulets of sweat ran down his face and the sides of his neck. His eyes kept darting over the fresh corpses that lay in grotesque shapes on the floor. The Brahmin bent and deliberately wiped the blade of his sword on his shirt. The man flinched, and his eyes darted furtively towards a wooden staircase at the back of the room, barely visible in the dark. The Brahmin turned on his heel, Antochlius behind him. Protesting and sobbing, the landlord followed them upstairs into a long corridor. Rooms ran along its length. Below, they could hear loud, excited squeaks and the sound of hundreds of clawed feet scurrying across the floor, as rats swarmed the fresh corpses. Unmoved, the Brahmin urged the landlord on, till he stopped at a door. The spymaster ignored the pleading eyes looking up him and thrust the man aside, then hammered on the door with the hilt of his sword.

'Open in the name of the king,' he demanded. Instantly the door was flung open by a bald, aging man who glared belligerently at the visitors. Two naked little boys lay on a dishevelled bed behind him. The Brahmin's eyes filled with disgust.

'Aren't you a shreshthin?' he asked. 'If I remember right, you were fined twenty gold coins for hoarding grain a few months ago.'

The man nodded, his eyes widening. He had recognized the Brahmin. 'It was just a rumour. A man in my position has many enemies…'

'Don't you have a young daughter who is to be married to one of the court scribes? A serious young man with curly hair? The king was pleased. If he knows that you like brothel boys, I doubt he will continue to be pleased,' the spymaster said.

The merchant's face crumpled. He fell at the Brahmin's feet and tried to clasp his ankles. The two boys, barely twelve or thirteen, huddled on the bed, round-eyed. The Brahmin wrinkled his nose and stepped back.

'Get up, we won't speak of this for now,' he said.

He turned to the landlord, who stood with his head hanging low on his chest.

'Are there boys in all the rooms?' he asked.

The man nodded with trepidation. The Brahmin glanced questioningly at Antochlius, who whispered something in the landlord's ear.

'The last room,' he said mournfully.

The Brahmin strode towards the end of the corridor and knocked on the door.

'Who is it? Go away. We don't want any more of your filthy wine,' a familiar voice shouted.

He knocked again, louder.

'Didn't I say, go away?' This time the voice sounded even gruffer. 'I don't pay you so much to be disturbed in the middle of the night.'

The Brahmin kicked open the door, shattering the flimsy wood. He walked in and bowing low, said, 'It's a pleasure to see you, prime minister.'

He turned to the young Greek who had leapt up from the bed, the sheets falling off his magnificently muscled, naked body. As he reached for the xiphos on a nearby table, the Brahmin warned softly, 'I wouldn't do that if I were you.'

'Put it down, Telemachus,' Radhagupta snapped. 'Don't you recognize the Brahmin?'

The Greek's arm froze. The sword remained untouched beside a bowl of grapes and a jug of wine. Two naked young boys gathered up their clothes and swiftly ran out.

'I'm sorry I intruded on your orgy, but I'm leaving now. You should too. Shall I offer my services as an escort? Narak Nagari is a dangerous place, although something tells me you are familiar with it, prime minister,' the Brahmin said politely.

He didn't miss the fury in his enemy's eyes.

'There is no need for that. My guards are downstairs,' Radhagupta answered ungraciously.

'I didn't see any,' said the Brahmin.

'Did you think I would be so foolish as to come here accompanied by soldiers dressed in the king's livery? They have come disguised as common folk.'

'Oh, but they didn't tell me, not one of them,' the Brahmin said, shaking his head regretfully. 'I suspect I've killed them all.'

Stupefied, the prime minister turned towards Telemachus, who had blanched at the spymaster's words. They had brought along ten men; seasoned warriors who had served in the Nalanda wars – some of them had even fought with Alexander in Persia and in the freezing valleys of Gandhara.

'Come, soldier, let's leave together. I think we should be a match for any thug in this city of murderers,' the Brahmin said.

He heard Telemachus's swift intake of breath as the Greek looked past his shoulder at Antochlius, who had stepped into the room.

'You!' they exclaimed simultaneously as recognition dawned.

'Traitor!' Telemachus shouted, his hand reaching for his sword again. Radhagupta barked a sharp command and Telemachus pulled back, though his eyes remained fixed on Antochlius.

'I thought you were injured,' Antochlius said. 'I came to rescue you, but now I find...'

He stopped in mid-sentence. There had been no fight here. There was no wounded Greek soldier. The Chief Eunuch had meant for Radhagupta to be found in the brothel. It was his way of giving the Brahmin leverage, the oldest weapon in spycraft. A favour for the future.

The Brahmin stood aside courteously. 'Prime minister, after you, of course. We are right behind you. You can sit behind my man on his horse. It may be a bit uncomfortable, with two people on one saddle, but I'm sure you will manage. And you, Greek,' he turned to Telemachus. 'You walk.'

The expression on Radhagupta's face was that of a trapped animal.

'And don't go near my horse, he is a bit skittish,' warned the Brahmin. 'He just killed a man, which may have whetted his appetite. He is a warhorse after all.'

Radhagupta looked stricken.

As they rode back with the prime minister perched uncomfortably behind Antochlius, and the Greek soldier loping along behind, the Brahmin pretended not to notice the hostile looks Telemachus threw at his fellow Greek. When they reached the gates of Pataliputra, the sky was growing lighter. Radhagupta dismounted.

'Don't bother to escort me further,' he said stiffly. Some of his hauteur had returned. 'I'm going to summon my carriage.'

The Brahmin gave a mocking salute and turned his horse around. As Antochlius did the same, Telemachus said to him, 'Why did you do this?'

'I was told you were hurt and needed help,' Antochlius said defensively.

'I don't believe you. If Amnestius saw you now, he would call you a disgrace to his noble name, watching his son betray another Greek.'

'Leave my father out of this,' Antochlius snapped.

'And all this while I thought you were my friend,' Telemachus said furiously.

'Spies have no friends,' the Brahmin interrupted. 'You should know that, being Radhagupta's spy yourself.'

Telemachus bit down his retort and strode past the guards.

'We'll have to keep an eye on him,' Antochlius warned.

The Brahmin nodded. Watching came easy to him. But it had been a day well spent, thanks to the Chief Eunuch's tip. Radhagupta was the most powerful man in the country after Ashoka. And now the Brahmin was in possession of a secret that could cause him real damage. Antochlius had done his job well.

A Veil of Deception

Antochlius was nowhere to be found when the spymaster reached the Ministry of Secrets to keep his appointment with his spy. His heart skipped a beat when he thought of the girl who was supposed to leave for Ujjain that night. Had she been captured by her enemies? Had her mysterious companion betrayed her? He looked around and found no signs of a struggle. Had they been attacked, Antochlius would not have surrendered quietly. That thought gave him relief. The pale night had entered its second hour. He stepped quickly into the Garden of Secrets through its vine-covered bower gate and walked towards the pavilion at its centre. Huge oak trees, planted equidistantly, probably during Chandragupta's time, interrupted the straight lines of well-pruned hedges.

'You can show yourself now,' he called sharply.

Hao stepped out from behind an oak, like a shadow come to life, and led him towards a moon clock behind the pavilion. A cloaked form lay on the freshly cut grass. A crossbow bolt protruded from its back.

'Is it Antochlius? Is he dead?' the spymaster asked.

'No. It's the Chief Eunuch,' Hao replied. 'Murdered.'

The Brahmin frowned. This was not meant to happen.

'You knew he had escaped from prison, didn't you?' Hao asked. 'Did you have a hand in it?'

'It's a long story. I caught him trying to flee Pataliputra

after escaping from the Palace of Hell. He had been hiding in his favourite opium den, waiting for the king's search parties to finish combing the area. The owner of the den is my man. I watched the eunuch creep into the palace, late at night, to take the gold he had stashed in his room before leaving for good. He was useful to me, perhaps too useful, and it cost him his life. Where the hell is Antochlius?'

'Gone. I found this on a bench in the pavilion, weighted down with a pebble. It's a message from him.' Hao held out a piece of parchment.

The Brahmin scanned it quickly. 'Dear Master, I saw the Chief Eunuch killed. It's dangerous for us to wait here anymore, so I'm leaving immediately with the women. I will meet you in Ujjain. Signed, your faithful servant Antochlius.'

He gave a sigh of relief, pleased that his spy had done the right thing, making a mental note to reward him. In that instant, something whistled past his ear. He seized Hao by the waist and flung her down. They hit the ground rolling, towards the protection of a thick hedge behind the pavilion, just as another projectile embedded itself next to them on the grass. The Brahmin cursed. The killer's aim was getting better. He lifted his head cautiously and peered at the bower gate. It teemed with shadows.

He ducked again as another projectile struck, missing him by the breadth of a hair. Crossbow bolts, he realized. The assassin was clearly someone trained by Alexander's master archers, who had used crossbows to devastating effect during the legendary Siege of Tyre, a few years before the Greek invader reached India. They were constructed following ancient methods with torque spring bundles that despatched lighter arrows over a longer distance than Magadha's bamboo bows could.

The Brahmin glanced at Hao. Her mouth was set in a grim line. He picked up a brick from the base of the hedge and pitched it a few feet away from their position. A hail of crossbow bolts thudded into the trees to their left. The two spies swiftly sprang up and dived behind a giant oak close by. Bolts slammed into its trunk, their force chipping away pieces of bark. When the Brahmin raised his head, he noticed Hao had slipped away, using the hedge as cover. He cursed and pondered his next move. It was a matter of time before the killer closed in.

There was a sudden silver flash behind the bower gate, a short sharp cry, and then he saw a cloaked form stumble through the leafy covering and fall to the ground. Hao stepped out from behind the vines, a long, thin knife in her hand.

The dead man lay at an unnatural angle, his head almost severed from his neck, his mouth open in stunned disbelief. The Brahmin knelt beside the body. A composite crossbow and a few bolts lay next to it.

Alexander's armies had brought such crossbows to India. Their long range and the skill of the archers had defeated the tribes of Hindu Kush and Gandhara, who had retaliated with spears, arrows and sling shots from crevasses high above the narrow mountain trails which led down into the plains. It was a feat no invader had achieved before.

The Brahmin inspected the strange weapon. Its handle

was sawed off, making it easy to hide under a cloak. Hao knelt next to the body and let out a low whistle. 'What do we have here?' she exclaimed, picking up a kovidara that had fallen from the pocket of the dead man's cloak.

'The Blood Flower?' the Brahmin asked incredulously, looking at the corpse. 'You've killed the Blood Flower?'

'I doubt it. This man didn't have the brains,' Hao replied. 'The Blood Flower would have killed the eunuch before you came to the garden, taken his cloak, hidden his body under a hedge and played dead, waiting for us. Our throats would have been slit the moment we reached him.'

From her pocket, she pulled out a crumpled muslin veil trimmed with delicate gold threads.

'I found this on the body,' she said. 'Its scent is unique.'

The Brahmin took it from her and inhaled deeply.

'Only one person wears this perfume,' Hao continued. 'The queen.'

The Brahmin was silent for a moment.

Then he turned on his heel and snapped, 'We need to see the king, and we need to see him now! Come, he must be in his apartments, going over his war plans.'

'No, he is with Lord Suma, the Kalingan ambassador, in the throne room,' Hao responded as she matched his gait.

He shot her a sideways look tinged with exasperation, She returned his look, one eyebow arched, as they hurried towards the king's seat. There was very little the Brahmin's favourite spy didn't know about the goings on in the palace. And her master knew it.

A Conspiracy to Murder

The sentries outside Ashoka's throne room in the judicial wing of the palace crossed their spears with a loud clash. Then, recognizing the Brahmin and Hao, they bowed and let them enter.

Ashoka received visiting dignitaries and ordinary people for a few hours in the morning and evening, seated on his throne in a great hall that could easily accommodate a thousand people. To reach him, the visitor had to pass a gigantic elephant shackled beside a flight of massive steps, trained by its mahout to raise its trunk and trumpet a welcome if the guest happened to be of exalted rank. Ahead of it, a gaggle of wild looking men and beggars blocked the way, pretending to be soldiers, breaking into shrieks and dance at the approach of a first-time visitor, who would be suitably disconcerted.

The Brahmin wondered how Lord Suma, Kalinga's envoy to Magadha, would have reacted to these strange sights. Calmly, perhaps? He was an enemy not to be underestimated.

Massive glass chandeliers hung from the hall's painted ceiling, spreading the light of hundreds of lamps burning in their copper receptacles. Silver torches planted in stone sconces gave additional light. Suma was seated on a low-backed silver stool at the foot of Ashoka's imposing throne, which stood on a tall stone platform covered with richly embroidered Persian carpets. Radhagupta stood beside him like a malevolent familiar. Suma was speaking in low tones to Ashoka, who sat drinking from a goblet of wine kept on a table at his elbow. He looked up at the sudden entrance of the spies. Suma turned to follow the king's gaze and gave a reptilian smile upon seeing the Brahmin.

The Kalingan ambassador was a short man with a secretive face and an enormous paunch, which strained at the buttons of his tunic. He smiled a lot, although his eyes remained cold. He was dressed in a long silver-trimmed shirt that reached his knees, tight linen trousers and Persian slippers. A serpent-shaped gold bracelet with tasselled red braids adorned his right wrist. 'A token of safe passage,' Suma said in a surprisingly thin voice, raising his arm for the Brahmin to see. 'This allows our diplomats unhindered travel through the kingdom. I've heard so much about you, nameless one. You must visit us. In Kalinga, you are a legend.' Suma's gaze was malicious.

The Brahmin was used to being hated. Sometimes, he even liked it. Bracelet or not, his men followed the movements of all the Kalingan diplomats, kidnapping and ruthlessly murdering any suspected of spying on Magadha. He was aware that even as parleys spoke peace in the shadow of war, Kalinga's commander-in-chief, General Nandidevi, was mobilizing his army of 60,000 trained infantry, 1,000 horses and 700 war elephants. His navy was strong too. A large flotilla of Kalingan warships guarded the eastern coastline, where Magadha was expected to launch its first naval offensive in case war broke out. Manipura city, which stood on the banks of the Brahmini river where it met the sea, forming a natural harbour, would be their point of entry. Kalingapatanam, the capital which lay further south, was also vulnerable.

Kalinga had been wary of its gigantic neighbour since Chadragupta's attempted invasion over fifty years ago. Its navy constantly patrolled the coast. A hundred-strong fleet of warships, drawn up in a concentric crescent formation, guarded both Manipura and Kalingapatanam. Flotillas of three-masted ships built with wood from the northern Mahakantara forests protected the ingress.

The sarvamandiras, used by both navies, with long cabins extending across their entire length, and powered by a thousand oarsmen, were fearsome weapons in their own right. Any one of them could hold a small army.

The smaller agramandiras were the main battleships. On their prows, master craftsmen had carved the heads of lions, buffaloes, serpents, elephants, tigers and demons to intimidate the enemy. They carried archers whose fire-arrows were tipped with a paste made of saltpetre and coal. From their decks, huge catapults operated by firemasters hurled explosive clay bombs filled with sulphur, charcoal and saltpetre at enemy ships, causing death and devastation.

On the Brahmini's northern bank stood Rajhagarh, King Srutayush's seaside palace. Theoretically Ashoka's navy could mount a surprise raid when Srutayush was in residence and take him hostage. However, landing Magadhan troops on the Manipura coast would not be easy.

Ashoka also knew that capturing Manipura would not be enough for him to win the battle against Kalinga. He would have to seize all the ports along the Kalinga coast to land his troops for a multi-pronged push inward. For this, he did not have enough vessels yet. New ships were being built in heavily guarded shipyards away from prying eyes, but it would be a while before they were battle ready.

The Magadhan army, on the other hand, had 600,000 infantry, 130,000 cavalry, and 9,000 elephants attended by 36,000 men, with thousands of chariots and charioteers, all functioning under six division commanders.

The Brahmin was aware that Ashoka planned a land assault on Kalinga, to be followed by a naval bombardment of Kalingapatanam and Manipura to spread panic and cut off Srutayush's escape. He had earlier informed Ashoka that Nandidevi kept a swift urdhava ship at a secret harbour near Kalingapatanam, ready to sail with the boy-king upon his command. Three of his best spies had died to discover the ship's location and he had vowed that their deaths would not be in vain.

Now, four heavily armed madhyamandiras of the Magadhan navy waited out of sight of the harbour, ever ready to capture the Kalingan king and convey him to Pataliputra. The Brahmin imagined the huge ships bearing down on their prey in a horseshoe formation, war drums booming, conches blowing and the rhythmic thunder of soldiers beating their shields with their sword hilts pulsating in the air as the sea frothed and churned with the force of thousands of oars. A fearsome sight indeed.

Then again, perhaps Nandidevi knew that his escape vessel wasn't a secret any more and he had an alternative plan in place, the Brahmin mused. Espionage was a game of illusion and misdirection. Like Lord Suma's invitation to visit Kalinga. A deadly trick.

'I would be honoured to come to Kalinga,' the Brahmin told Suma. 'I've heard of the luxury and comfort of Kalingan ships and the skill of your sailors. Isn't a sarvamandira leaving soon for Kalingapatanam in the next two days from Pataliputra? Perhaps you mean to travel on it?'

Suma's eyes narrowed. 'And you know this how?' he asked.

The Brahmin shrugged.

'I'm impressed,' Suma said with a bark of a laugh. 'So, shall I inform the captain of the ship that you will be boarding it?'

'I have some urgent work to finish,' the spymaster replied. 'Once that's over, I'll be happy to come.'

'Can't your work wait? General Nandidevi is keen to meet you.'

'Your Excellency is most kind. What does a lowly court official like me have to offer the great Nandidevi?'

'It is said the great Chanakya trained you himself when you were just a boy. To have been chosen by him must mean that you were an extraordinary pupil.'

'Lord Suma's offer is a great opportunity for Magadha,' Radhagupta interrupted with a crafty smile, turning to Ashoka. 'Your Majesty, it was I who persuaded him to invite the Brahmin to Kalinga. His visit will strengthen the friendship and trust between our countries.'

By prompting the invitation, the prime minister had made his first move. The Brahmin suspected he had made a deal with Suma. Once he reached Kalinga, he was certain he would be thrown into a dungeon for some imagined crime and executed. A victory for both Radhagupta and Nandidevi, who would be equally relieved to be rid of him. The general knew that Ashoka would invade, no matter what. And he needed every possible advantage to keep Kalinga from falling.

The Brahmin wondered what Radhagupta had demanded in return for his death. Given time, he would find out, but time was something he did not have.

'The king has a few errands for me,' the Brahmin told Suma. 'After I finish those, I'll be delighted to visit Kalinga.'

A taut silence descended on the room. Then Ashoka nodded.

'Yes, I do have some work for him.' He turned towards Suma. 'I'm sure he will finish it soon. Won't you, Brahmin?'

The spymaster bowed. He noticed the disappointment on Suma's face. This is a man I will have to watch carefully, he thought. He wants me out of the way at any cost.

'Our king is very young,' Suma said, injecting a note of regret into his voice. 'He would learn much from a man like you.'

'I am a man of little knowledge, but what I have is at your king's disposal,' the Brahmin replied with a courtesy that did not come easily.

'Then everything is settled,' Suma said, grinning widely and rubbing his hands together. The Brahmin did not miss the satisfied expression in Radhagupta's eyes.

He was now certain that the two men were in league with each other. The invitation to Kalinga was Radhagupta's revenge for humiliating him in Narak Nagari. Years of instinct, honed by working in the shadows, warned him that a conspiracy was afoot. He needed Ashoka's trust. And he needed it now. He made his next move carefully.

'I'll gladly meet your king and his general,' he said. 'Once I'm there, we could arrange some mock war games too. That would be a suitable way of showing off the battle prowess of your kingdom.'

Suma's eyes widened in dismay at the Brahmin's words. Mock war games were usually conducted with the help of large maps that had been carved on polished wooden boards. Painted wooden blocks representing formations of cavalry, infantry and the navy were moved around to imitate battles and explore different outcomes. Inevitably they revealed the strategic thinking and capabilities of those engaged in the game.

'As King Ashoka's representative, I naturally hope to see the Kalingan army and navy at their exercises, too,' he continued. 'I'm sure I'll be suitably impressed.'

The king smiled broadly. 'Then it's all arranged,' he said.

The Brahmin looked at Suma. 'I hear pirates are plaguing your fishing villages,' he said.

Suma nodded reluctantly and replied, 'Just a few here

and there, but we have fast Dirghika ships patrolling the coast. We managed to catch and hang most of them. Some of the pirates were from Magadha,' he added.

Ashoka stroked his chin contemplatively.

'The Brahmin will leave for your kingdom in six days,' he announced.

'Your Majesty is kind,' Suma answered cautiously. 'I'll wait until the Nameless One is ready.'

'That's good. But I cannot allow you both of you to leave Pataliputra unprotected,' Ashoka said. 'Three of my best warships, an Agramandira and two Madhyamandiras, will escort you to Kalingapatanam. After all, we can't have pirates, especially from Magadha, attacking a ship that is carrying King Srutayush's envoy, can we? My ships will dock at your harbour until my man returns.'

The Brahmin heard Hao's faint sigh of relief.

'He is under our protection,' Suma said weakly. 'We are very capable of looking after him, Your Majesty.'

The king ignored this and indicated that the audience was over. As Suma bowed himself out, Ashoka sat back and let out a great whoop, his whole body convulsed with laughter. His head was thrown back and the row of even, white polished teeth shone cruelly in the light of the torches.

'I thank you for your intervention, sire,' the Brahmin murmured.

'What if I hadn't intervened? Would you have gone with Lord Suma without a guard?'

The Brahmin shrugged.

'Who knows, my lord? Perhaps Lord Suma himself

would not have reached Kalingapatanam. From what I hear, the road to the harbour runs through a forest which is full of dacoits and murderers.'

The king's eyes narrowed. 'That would have been most unfortunate, for both Magadha and Kalinga.'

'Not as unfortunate as for me, Your Majesty,' the Brahmin replied caustically.

Ashoka laughed and took a huge draught of wine.

The Brahmin cleared his throat. 'But there are more important things than the safety of my person, sire,' he said.

'Like?' the king asked, amused.

The Brahmin took a moment to gather his thoughts, then said, 'I've discovered a plot, sire, which directly involves the palace. I believe that unless it is foiled immediately, our enemies will get the opening they need to foment unrest in the kingdom.'

A distant gong announced that it was time for ablutions in the harem.

The Brahmin was aware that upon him rested the safety of the kingdom and its people, who were unaware of the endless war being fought in the shadows.

'Magadha is not safe, sire,' the Brahmin said. 'You are not safe.'

Ashoka reached for his wine cup again, grunting.

'It is your job to keep us safe,' he said. 'And you have six days left to prove it.'

'Then listen to me, sire,' the Brahmin replied. 'There has been another death in the palace.'

The Sign of the Blood Flower

Ashoka sat quietly for a moment. His eyes glittered like polished black stones from the northern provinces. Carefully he placed the goblet of wine on the table and raised an interrogative eyebrow.

The Brahmin said softly, 'I found the body of the Chief Eunuch in the garden of the Ministry of Secrets, sire. He was killed with a crossbow bolt to the back.'

He left out the part where he had surprised the eunuch in his chamber, surreptitiously counting coins in the dark.

'That's impossible!' the king said tersely, disbelief writ large on his face. 'Nobody can escape the Palace of Hell. Nobody can take Girika's victims from him.'

The Brahmin knew this was the opening he sought.

'Perhaps the prime minister knows the truth. He was seen with Girika around the time that the eunuch disappeared,' he said.

Radhagupta did not exhibit any signs of unease at this pronouncement, as if he had been expecting it all along. He told Ashoka respectfully, 'I was in the Palace of Hell to oversee preparations for the eunuch's interrogation when Girika's attendant came in and whispered in his ear. I couldn't hear what he said. Girika left abruptly, promising to be back in an hour. I became suspicious then and decided to shadow him. I followed him to a tavern just outside the palace gate. I hid behind the gatehouse and waited, but nobody showed up. Certain now that something was amiss, I revealed myself to Girika. We rushed back to his chambers, but by then, the eunuch had escaped.'

'How dare you keep such a matter secret from me? And how did that creature escape from a heavily guarded prison?' Ashoka thundered.

'I immediately ordered a citywide search. I was sure he would be caught soon and didn't want to tell you until I had him. We learned that just after Girika had rushed off, a stranger had arrived at the prison gates with orders to take the eunuch to you. The guards were shown the royal seal, so he was released.'

'Someone shows up with a fake message and a forged seal and you lose an important prisoner?' Ashoka shouted, his dark brows gathering like a thunderstorm on his wide forehead. He leaped up from his throne and smacked Radhagupta's cheek with the flat of his palm. The prime minister almost lost his balance.

'You were ordered to get the eunuch's confession, but you let him get away instead. And now he is dead.'

Ashoka turned to the Brahmin. 'Spymaster, find out who did this, or by Lord Shiva's trident, both you and Radhagupta will be roasting on Girika's Couch of Misery even before your seven days are over.'

He pointed at Hao.

'She is your fox as you are my wolf. Bring me the eunuch's killer.'

'He is dead. Hao killed him,' the Brahmin answered.

'What! Why wasn't he captured instead? He would

have told us everything we need to know about my concubine's killer.'

'More important matters have come to light, my lord,' the Brahmin said. He held up the veil Hao had picked up in the garden.

'Would you smell it, please, sire?' he requested.

Ashoka raised the veil to his nose and inhaled deeply. Understanding dawned in his eyes.

'This belongs to the queen,' he said, confused. 'How did...'

In a flash Radhagupta moved to indicate the Brahmin.

'He must have planted it on the eunuch,' he snapped.

'Why would he do something so stupid?'

The prime minister's voice rose in response to Ashoka's question. 'I'm willing to wager he is working for Nandidevi, Your Majesty. He wants to involve the queen in a scandal so terrible that the people will rise up, accusing her of killing your concubine in a fit of jealousy. Maybe he killed the girl himself. Send him to Girika and we'll get the truth out of him in a day.'

So that was Radhagupta's game. To implicate him in the deaths.

But who had informed him of the Chief Eunuch's murder? He was already inside the throne room when Hao discovered the body.

The Brahmin's mind went back to the night before, when he had caught the eunuch creeping back into the palace for his money. The Brahmin had ordered his men to take him to the Ministry of Secrets through a secret tunnel inside the palace to evade prying eyes. Here they had interrogated the eunuch about the concubine's murder. He had been told to hide there until Antochlius arrived with the girls. They were then to leave for Ujjain where the queen would protect them. The Brahmin needed the eunuch to expose Radhagupta's connivance with Lord Suma.

But now, it seemed to him that someone must have been standing there in the darkness as he instructed his spies to take the eunuch away; probably a Kalingan spy who had followed him and killed him before he could meet Antochlius. Or had him killed. Someone who had a lot to lose. Or gain, depending on the perspective. But who could it have been?

The concubine's murderer?

The Blood Flower?

Or Radhagupta himself?

And who was the women who had freed the eunuch from prison? He wouldn't say, even after being threatened during his interrogation. She seemed to fill him with fear.

The prime minister must have been waiting for the moment when Ashoka discovered that the eunuch's escape had been kept a secret from him. The Brahmin marvelled at his timing and political skill.

Ashoka gestured to Radhagupta to continue.

The prime minister resumed, 'After we found the eunuch had escaped, Girika subjected his assistant to torture. The wretch confessed that a woman had approached him on his way to work in the prison, and offered him two gold coins in return for sending Girika to the tavern. She told him a group of Kalingans was planning the king's assassination and Girika would be well rewarded if he captured them.'

The Brahmin raised his eyebrows in mock dismay.

'Her face was hidden by a black cowl. But he noticed her eyes. They slanted, like hers,' Radhagupta pointed at Hao.

Ashoka was sceptical. 'What would she gain by freeing the eunuch?'

'Perhaps the eunuch had discovered that the Brahmin, working for the Kalingans, had murdered the concubine to discredit the queen. The spymaster used trickery to free him and then killed him before he could reveal any of this under torture.'

'A serious allegation, were it not so contemptible,' the Brahmin scoffed.

He looked at the monarch and said, 'I appreciate that the prime minister is in a hurry to destroy me, my lord, but I had already informed you that Hao was on a mission to locate the Blood Flower. She couldn't have been in the Palace of Hell at the same time.'

Ashoka nodded.

'He is bluffing, my lord! He is trying to protect his bitch!' Radhagupta screamed, eyes blazing.

Ashoka stared at him without blinking. Radhagupta began to lose his newfound confidence, and started to squirm.

'You seem to know a lot about all this, Radhagupta. After all, the eunuch escaped while you were in the Palace of Hell,' Ashoka said. 'Maybe you are hiding something from me again. It's you I should send to Girika...'

'I've always been loyal to you, Your Majesty. But this man…' Radhagupta pointed at the Brahmin. 'Spies can't be trusted.'

'Yet, it's my prime minister who is in the habit of hiding information from his king,' Ashoka responded. 'Radhagupta, you are blinded by hatred for my spymaster. It interferes with your objectivity. My kingdom is in danger. Spies and assassins are everywhere, and we move on Kalinga in a few months. Now, a valuable prisoner has escaped. Instead of working against the Brahmin, why don't you work with him? I don't have to remind you the stakes are very high.'

From his pocket, the spymaster took out the kovidara retrieved from the assassin's pocket and informed the king of the circumstances.

'Your assistant killed the Blood Flower?' Ashoka was shocked. The Brahmin cleared his throat. 'Unfortunately not, Your Majesty. Look at the flower. It's faded, almost dead. The Blood Flower always uses a fresh kovidara to mark each murder.'

'Then how did this one…'

'I think the killer was pretending to be the Blood Flower, to confuse us. Or maybe the Blood Flower hired him for an impersonation. Either way, this killer knew I would be meeting Antochlius in the Garden of Secrets. In which case, there is an infiltrator at large in the palace, who wants us to believe we've killed the Blood Flower and let our guard down. An infiltrator who may also be the murderer of Your Majesty's concubine, waiting to strike again.'

The king took the veil and twisted it around his fingers, his brow knotted in concentration.

'First a kovidara is found with a glove, like one the queen favours. Now this!'

He abruptly flung the veil at the Brahmin. In a movement that defied the eye, Hao snatched it mid-air. The monarch laughed, his eyes uncharacteristically kind.

'What wouldn't I give for such loyalty! Perhaps she thought I hurled a knife at you.'

The Brahmin said nothing.

Ashoka continued, 'Danger is in the air, I can smell it. Go, Brahmin. Ride to Ujjain if you must.'

The Brahmin bowed.

'Wait! Here.' The king drew a golden ring from the third finger of his right hand. On it was mounted a huge ruby carved with the royal lion of Magadha. He gave it to the Brahmin.

'Wear this always. It gives you supreme authority over anyone and everything in the kingdom. You can kill in my name, question or arrest anyone, including the greatest of lords.'

'Anyone, Your Majesty?' the Brahmin asked, watching Ashoka's eyes go to the veil entwined in Hao's fingers. He did not miss the fleeting look of sadness, which was swiftly replaced by a steely resolve. He nodded.

'Yes, anyone,' he answered.

Radhagupta let out a startled yelp.

Once the Brahmin had left, Ashoka got up from his seat and placed an arm on the prime minister's shoulder. He said, 'I know you hate him because I trust him. One day the time will come when matters will be settled between you both. Perhaps it will end well for you, perhaps not, who knows…'

Radhagupta nodded slowly.

'O Radhagupta, I love you like I would an uncle, or an elder brother. You helped me become the king and have given me wise counsel against my enemies. I will always heed your words carefully…'

He stepped back and suddenly grabbed Radhagupta's tunic, yanking him forcefully towards himself. 'But if you pull another stunt like that and let an important prisoner escape just to frame a rival, I swear by my grandfather that my elephants will crush your head open like a ripe coconut.'

Radhgupta shivered. Summoning his courage, he asked the king, 'Do you love him that much, Your Majesty? Is that the reason you trust him?'

Ashoka took his seat on the throne again and took a long sip of wine. Wiping his mouth with the back of his hand, he belched lightly. 'No, because I love my kingdom the most, and there is nobody I trust to watch over it more than the Brahmin. He can protect it in a way none of you, not even my army, ever can.'

'How is that?' asked Radhagupta.

'Because the Brahmin's way is different,' answered the king. 'He is not like you or me. His is the way of the night.'

Radhagupta regarded the king in speculative silence. Ashoka looked back quizzically. The prime minister smiled, and the king thought he looked like a snake that had been biding its time in a garden of shadows.

'Maybe you won't need the Brahmin to protect the kingdom when you can do it better yourself. Let me tell you a story, Your Majesty,' Radhagupta whispered, his eyes Fda glittering with relish at the effect his words would soon have on his royal master. 'The story of a great war, a Buddhist monk and a princess.'

As he began to speak, Ashoka slipped into a trance, listening to his prime minister reveal a secret older than time itself.

An Unexpected Visitation

Hao woke, her senses on fire. A draught of cold air came in through the open window of her room at the inn where the Brahmin and she had halted for the night, on their way to Ujjain. She lay still, trying to calm her thundering heart. Never before had someone been able to get close to her without her knowing. In the darkness, she saw a figure standing over her, cloaked and hooded, its burning eyes fixed on her intensely.

'It's you,' Hao hissed.

The intruder pressed a finger to Hao's lips.

'Dao,' Hao whispered, removing the hand from her mouth.

'Dao is dead. She died long ago, as I told you before. You must stop looking for her.'

Hao shook her head without speaking. Tears welled up in her eyes. She felt the wetness on her cheeks with wonder, because she did not remember having cried for a very long time.

The intruder stroked her cheek gently, as if caressing a sleeping doe.

'It doesn't have to be like this,' Hao said, an uncharacteristically pleading note entering her voice.

The Blood Flower laughed softly and stepped away from her, and in the flicker of an eye, vanished through the open window into the night.

Double-cross

The dawn was early-dark when the Brahmin awoke. Within the hour, he had pulled on a white cambric shirt made with fabric brought from faraway Gaul, and tucked his black deer leather hose into a pair of soft Persian leather boots. Winter was around the corner. He draped his iron-studded baldric across his shoulder and buckled it at his waist. From it hung his great battle sword in its plain leather scabbard. He tied a thick, broad leather band around his neck for protection against enemy daggers, and fastened his black woollen riding cloak under his chin with a silver chain.

He found Hao waiting for him in the dining room, seated at a roughly hewn trestle table. A fire burned heartily in a large copper pan mounted on a tripod. Sparks scattered in the wind that flew in through the cracks in the large wooden door. A mangy dog of dubious parentage was curled upon a heap of sackcloth near the fire. It growled half-heartedly when the Brahmin entered, then went back to sleep with a long sigh. The storm lanterns hanging from the rafters creaked on their iron handles and swayed, shifting the shadows. A sleepy eyed attendant shuffled in, bearing on a tray several pieces of soft white flatbread and a dish of lamb cubes cooked in sour milk.

After breaking their fast, the two spies went down to the brick-paved courtyard where their horses waited, tied to square pegs driven into the ground. The remains of their morning meal – crushed wheat cooked in mutton fat – and fresh hay lay in their troughs. The animals snorted white plumes of warm breath into the cold air. Garuda whimpered impatiently, stomping on the stones. Hao's black stallion neighed with pleasure at the sight of his mistress, then stood still as she settled the saddle and tightened the girdle, looping it through a hanging iron hoop before letting down the stirrups. The animals, sensing the journey ahead and the tension of their riders, whinnied expectantly.

Both were huge Kamboja warhorses, known for their speed and fearlessness in battle, and trained by handlers from the eponymous kingdom situated in the far north-west of Magadha, beyond the mountains that separated Persia from the land of the Indus. The Kambojas – also called 'Ashvakas', meaning horsemen – were a tribe famed throughout the known world as the greatest mounted warriors and horse breeders ever. They often hired their cavalry out to warring kings as mercenaries.

As they mounted, the Brahmin glanced at Hao.

'Did you sleep with your window open?' he asked.

Hao felt her heart tremble. She raised an eyebrow suspiciously.

'You are sniffling. You must be careful. Someone might get into your room while you are asleep and slit your throat. What will I do then for an assistant?'

She gave a strangled smile and slapped her horse on its back. The animal leapt forward with a loud neigh and the Brahmin followed at a leisurely pace a few yards behind.

Ujjain was approximately 100 yojanas away, a ride of about eight days from Pataliputra. The Brahmin hoped it would take them only five days, since they were used to sleeping on horseback. Five days were all he had left to solve the murders, counting the Chief Eunuch's. The horses trotting at a regulated pace, were trained to ride long distances with little rest. He gently urged Garuda forward to keep pace with Hao. The roads of the kingdom were kept in good condition. Chandragupta had learnt from Chanakya the importance of maintaining these veins of commerce, which made the kingdom rich. Bindusara had extended them further and Ashoka had invested in building even wider and smoother roads.

The dawn opened slowly, suffusing the endless green fields with ghostly mist. The Ganga flowed beyond the endless grid of paddy fields, feeding the rich alluvial soil of the river basin. Boats carrying muslin and silk from the eastern territories, and iron and copper excavated from mines across the kingdom, travelled to Pataliputra in an endless stream. War was in the air, but all they could see around them was the peaceful countryside. The codes of war were strict and mercilessly enforced. No peasant was to be harmed, no women were to be raped or abducted, nor any property stolen. Merchant caravans travelling to and from Pataliputra were left undisturbed and they often shared food and wine with soldiers on the march. The merchants were grateful for their company because travelling through the forests was dangerous, although Ashoka's law keepers showed dacoits and outlaws no leniency when apprehended.

In Bindusara's time, the forest had almost reached the gates of Pataliputra. Ashoka had cleared vast tracts of land by cutting down thousands of trees. The timber was used in the construction of forts, palaces and the houses of rich merchants. The cleared land was given to farmers for free. Ashoka had inherited a prosperous kingdom, where trade and commerce flourished. Traders borrowed from the state treasury to expand their business and paid interest, thus swelling the royal coffers. The Brahmin knew that Radhagupta helped tradesmen get loans at cheaper rates, and profited from the deals by extracting bribes. The merchants then loaned the borrowed money to the needy at very high interest, with a part of the profits going to the prime minister. Radhagupta also owned many iron mines and was said to be one of the richest men in the kingdom.

'The night before he died, the Chief Eunuch told me about the deal Radhagupta has made with Lord Suma,' the Brahmin told Hao.

'Then why didn't you tell Ashoka?'

'It wasn't the right time, Hao. I need more proof than just a dead fugitive's words.'

'Then let's unstrike the deal,' Hao laughed.

'Indeed, let us,' the Brahmin replied.

A hare darted out from under a hedge and sped across their path. Hao swore and reined in her horse. The Brahmin laughed as he passed her. Cursing, she caught up with him. They trotted past a farmer in his field, coaxing his oxen to pull an iron sheared plough, which furrowed deep quadrangles in the moist earth.

The smell of the forest reached them in the wind; a confection of flowers, newborn leaves and things ancient, unnamed and untamed.

'Radhagupta expects the Kalingans to seize me when I reach Kalingapatanam. Perhaps torture me for information on Ashoka's war plans. After which Radhagupta will denounce me as a traitor. Even if I manage to escape, I'll be tainted in Ashoka's eyes,' the Brahmin said.

'Will Ashoka believe him?'

'I don't know. But Ashoka is paranoid. He likes to believe the worst of everyone but expects the best. Suma is playing both sides. He knows it's a matter of time before Magadha invades Kalinga. General Nandidevi doesn't stand a chance. You know our king. He wants Kalinga, and doesn't care how many men die for it. He is willing to sacrifice hundreds, if not thousands, of his soldiers. He wants to succeed where his grandfather failed. He wants to prove to the world and to himself that he is greater than the great Chandragupta who defeated Alexander.'

'And then?'

'Once I am dead, Ashoka will need a new spymaster. Radhagupta would have promised Suma the job. He will tell Ashoka that the court will need someone who knows Kalinga well. After the annexation, there will be enough Kalingan nobles and lords who stand to lose their lands and positions at court and are ready to rebel. To identify and capture them, Ashoka will need someone like Suma.'

'But on what charge will they arrest you and throw you in prison? You are Ashoka's representative after all.'

'Nandidevi is ambitious. What if something were to happen to the boy-king? They will blame it on me and Ashoka will be forced to disown me.'

'Do you think he knows of Radhagupta and Suma's plot? You are his loyal spymaster and have exposed so many such conspiracies against his kingdom and his life, more times than I care to remember.'

The Brahmin sighed. 'Kings have no loyalties. That's why they are kings.'

Hao shivered and drew her cloak around her. The Brahmin guessed she was feeling more than just the chill of winter.

'Let's hope it doesn't come to that, little falcon. It's not that easy to get rid of me.' The Brahmin smiled grimly.

'Speaking of torture, I learned something interesting just before I left Pataliputra,' Hao said. 'Monks are being tortured for information about a new prophet who walks the path of the Buddha. Radhagupta and the Brahmins fear a fresh challenge to their power – the Buddha's teachings have become extremely popular. Buddhist monks have been travelling through the kingdom for years now, preaching the middle path, which is angering the Brahmins.'

The spymaster was aware of the power struggle between the Brahmins of Magadha and the Buddha's followers. He had heard of the prince turned prophet, born before Chandragupta's time in a distant mountain kingdom, who taught the principles of Dhamma, the true faith. King Bindusara was so impressed by the discipline and selflessness of the wandering monks that he had allowed them to build monasteries in his kingdom. The Buddha himself was reputed to have performed miracles when he was alive, healing the sick, curing barren women and reviving parched fields.

'If the Buddha is dead, who is the new prophet?' the Brahmin asked.

'I hear talk of a new Master who follows the Buddha's path. His followers have an incredible threshold of pain, as Girika has discovered recently,' Hao said. 'But one of them finally broke under torture and told him that a princess from Lanka has arrived in Magadha with a secret weapon. A weapon with the power to end the world. The king who has the weapon will win the war.'

'How do you know that?'

'There is little that happens in Pataliputra I don't know about,' Hao replied.

'Then did you know we're being followed?' the Brahmin asked.

'That too,' Hao replied. A lone rider was trailing them from afar, moving through the morning mist like a persistent ghost. The two spies slowed their horses. Their pursuer did the same. They accelerated their pace, and the figure urged his horse forward, but retained the distance between them.

'Do you think it's an agent of Suma's?' Hao asked.

'Or Radhagupta's. Both must hope we will lead them to the Golden Scythe.'

'They will double-cross each other if either of them gets their hands on it. If it is Kalinga, Suma's deal with Radhagupta to replace me will be off. The weapon will obliterate Magadha.'

'If all goes well, we'll be the ones who get the Golden Scythe. Meanwhile, if spies are on our trail, we have to warn the queen.'

'Before or after you ask her about the veil from the garden?' Hao laughed.

The Brahmin sighed. Questioning Queen Asandhimitra would take a lot of tact. She would not reveal anything she did not wish to. Showing her Ashoka's ring was sure to invite her fury and he had no desire to anger the powerful queen. He knew she liked him; there was something unsaid between them. The search for the murderer of the concubine was becoming very complicated, he thought.

The two spies urged their mounts to a gallop towards the waiting forest. Their pursuer spurred his horse forward too.

'An ambush would not be entirely unexpected,' the Brahmin observed.

'I agree,' replied Hao, feeling the buckle of her sword belt.

When they turned to look, the horseman had disappeared.

A Slaying in the Forest

The party of three heavily veiled women protected by Antochlius, which had left the Garden of Secrets the night before, split into two. A contingent of cavalry comprising battle-hardened Greeks was awaiting them at a fork in the road. Two of the three women took the highway to Ujjain under armed escort. Antochlius and another took the other route as he had been instructed by the Brahmin, which led away through the forest, past small towns and wayside villages. He believed this would confuse her pursuers, who would expect her to be heavily guarded.

The road they took was narrow and unpaved in places, rutted by the wheels of oxcarts and passing through dense forest where ambushes were common. But Antochlius had confidence in his ability to ward off any foolhardy band of ruffians who dared to take on a highly trained member of the palace guard. Besides, he would be meeting his master soon on the way.

As they rode on, it seemed as though the entire country was preparing for war. Soldiers were everywhere. Their passes were checked at gateposts along the way. An archer on the lookout tower of a town gave a low whistle at the sight of the girl, who sat slim and erect on her saddle. The road to Pataliputra had been widened by Bindusara to enable caravans from the various ports in the west to travel in comfort. There were caravanserais along the route, with comfortable rooms and plenty of food and wine. Many merchants travelled from the port of Broach, carrying porcelain, fine muslin, Greek wine and articles of brass and tin to the capital city. At the inns where Antochlius and his companion stopped, they were met with curious glances from landlords and customers alike, the men trying to get a glimpse of the girl's face behind her veil. Serving wenches reported that she kept largely to herself, ate in her room and summoned them only when absolutely necessary – but all the time wearing her veil. One of them surprised her praying to the Buddha, and declared her beautiful and aristocratic.

Three days later, the two reached the outskirts of Ujjain. After a good night's sleep at a roadside lodge, they continued their journey along the Shipra river, which flowed towards Ujjain, wide and deep. The city was close by, but still a day's ride through the forest ahead. In the distance temple bells sang melodious praise of Shiva, the presiding deity. They passed Mahakal temples where priests were performing bhasm-aartis, smearing the Shivalings with hot ash from burning pyres by the riverbank.

'Your rituals are bizarre,' the girl said.

'You mean those of Magadha, surely?' Antochlius laughed. 'My father, Aeimnestus, came to Magadha from Macedonia.'

'All of you, from Greece or Magadha, do strange things in the name of the gods. Fighting bulls, taking ashes from corpses, sitting naked in the snowy mountains of the north. It's madness.'

'Then what is sane, prin –'

She silenced him with a sharp look.

'The Buddha's way is different,' she said. Her voice had softened, taking on a dreamy quality.

She closed her eyes, and Antochlius saw her blinking back tears.

'Missing home?' he asked gently.

She nodded silently, thinking of her father's home, its large, cool, perfumed rooms and rectangular courtyards lined with flowerbeds. She missed the Buddhist shrine in the middle of the main palace courtyard, sheltered by a venerable tree. It was said that the tree had been planted by a great Brahmin king who had been killed in a terrible war, at a time when the gods walked the earth. She missed the benevolent, golden statue of the Buddha with its meditative smile. She wanted to lie by the lotus pool in the prayer garden, its still, green surface shining like an enigmatic mirror, reflecting answers to questions yet to be asked. She sighed.

'Don't worry, you'll be home soon,' he said, prodding his powerful Nisean stallion to a slow trot.

The girl sat on a Kathiawari roan, which she now brought alongside Antochlius. They cantered along, listening to the river chanting its timeless mantra of passage. The cinnamon sky was beginning to lighten and a flock of bats flitted above, fleeing towards the caves, which lay hidden in the forest across the Shipra. The girl shivered.

'Bats! A bad omen,' she whispered.

'*Dhik tam cha tam cha madanam cha imam cha mam cha*!' Antochlius rattled off the words softly.

The girl gave him a confused look.

Antochlius responded, 'The bats are headed for the caves near the Gadkalika temple, where the great poet Bhartrihari lived once upon a time. He was a king who decided to become a hermit when his love life turned, shall we say, complicated. His favourite queen lusted after another man, who was besotted by a beautiful courtesan, who was in love with Bhartrihari. He left the palace, cursing. "*Dhik tam cha tam cha madanam cha imam cha mam cha*!"'

'Meaning?'

'Woe be to us all; she, her lover, the god of love, myself and the entire world.'

'What a strange story,' she said. 'Love can be so scary. But bats are scarier.'

Her voice was husky and low, with inflections of an alien accent. Antochlius was tempted to ask his young companion if she had ever been in love, but desisted, knowing it was not his place to question a highborn girl about her personal life. Instead, he smiled reassuringly and said, 'Don't worry, my lady. The Brahmin will take care of everything.'

'You speak of the Brahmin as if he were some omnipotent god.' She paused. 'I knew someone like him once, in my father's palace.'

'He is a man whom even the gods envy, for he would have been one of them had he not been born on this earth. People say he can hear and see everything and it is useless to hide from him. He can be everywhere, or wherever he wants to be, whenever – or so they say.'

'Old wives' tales,' the girl said with a teasing laugh, which was captured by the dancing loops of temple bells.

'The Brahmin knows everything. He will solve your predicament once we reach Ujjain. You'll be safe there with the queen,' Antochlius persisted.

'A lady I met in the harem told me they call Ujjain Prati Kalpa, which means it has been in existence since the beginning of the world,' the girl said. 'To me, it looks like the end of the world.'

A dog howled in the distance. Its lament was taken up by other dogs. 'A lady wearing black gloves?' Antochlius asked, half in jest. She shot him a warning look. The dogs took up their mournful song again. The girl shivered.

'First bats, now the howling of dogs. If my father's astrologers were here, they would ask me to return home immediately.'

'I don't believe in omens,' Antochlius said.

'What do you believe in then, Greek?'

'The Brahmin.'

The road left the riverbank and climbed up. As the riders crested a hill, they saw the land spread out below like ether imbued with silver. It slid along the hillsides far away, causing shadows to deepen and then grow faint as the cool light shepherded them along the forested slopes. Little pools bloomed with white water lilies. Wild flowers grew along the way. There were blue atasis the colour of Krishna's skin; golden tasselled karnikaras, red bandhooks associated with the sun god, Surya; and akundas, famed as one of the five arrows of Kamadeva, the god of love. Champaka trees filled the air with the heady fragrance of their ivory-coloured flowers. Bowers of malati gave off a jasmine-like perfume. When a pair of lovers stands beneath them, the flowers fall only on the head of the woman, Antochlius told the girl.

She gave a melodious laugh. 'You are quite romantic for a mercenary,' she remarked.

The Greek did not respond. He pointed at a fringe of flowers that grew along a large thicket with a slightly unsteady hand.

'Kovidara,' he said.

'They look pretty – red and fat,' said the girl.

The Greek was silent for a moment. Then he said slowly, 'You don't understand. These are raktapushpas – blood flowers. Haven't you heard about an assassin by the same name? Rumour is that this killer is in Pataliputra to assassinate the king.'

The girl reined in her horse, her gaze steely. Antochlius felt the power of her royal blood, born to command.

'Are you trying to frighten me, Antochlius?' she asked.

He shook his head. 'Mercenaries and spies have no compunctions about killing or wading into battle, but we are a superstitious lot,' he admitted. 'We also fight to conquer fear.'

The girl clucked her tongue and nudged her roan at a steady trot towards a clearing in the woods.

'Let me go first,' Antochlius offered. 'Up ahead is the spot where we are expected to meet my master. And remember, if he is not there and things go sideways, you are to ride for Ujjain.'

'Yes, I know. He told me,' she said tartly.

Antochlius spurred his horse forward, then stopped suddenly and cursed. He shouldn't have been riding alongside her. He should have been in the lead, alert for any ambush. But it was too late. They could hear the thunder of approaching hooves and in the next moment, a group of horsemen was pelting towards them, weapons raised. They were in black, and masked; leather armour protected their chests and bellies. Their legs were encased in tall black leather boots with jangling spurs, pushed into stirrups.

Antochlius made some swift calculations in his head, gauging the distance between them and the highway to Ujjain. Satisfied, he yelled to the girl, 'Flee, my lady! Ride! Make for the highway, while I hold off these rogues until the master arrives. The convoy we parted from at the crossroads cannot be far, since the carriage is too large to move fast. The guards will protect you.'

He drew his sword and dug his heels forcefully into the sides of his horse. It leaped forward. From the corner of his eye, he saw the girl draw out a long, thin rapier from her saddlebag.

'No, no, there are too many of them. Ride as fast as you can and find the soldiers. I'll catch up with you soon,' he shouted, though he already knew it was a lie.

She gave a quick nod and spurred her roan through the trees.

'After her!' shouted a short, paunchy man in a silver-trimmed tunic. He was on a light ornamental chariot practically pureed in gold and silver, drawn by two white horses with colourful feathered plumes on their heads.

It was unlike the four- or six-wheeled war machines of the Magadhan army.

'Charge! Charge! Faster, faster! Kill the king's man!' the little man screeched to his cohorts, almost leaping up and down on his seat and waving a small dagger. A serpent bracelet with tasselled red braids glinted on his wrist. Beside him sat a tall, fair, slender woman, dressed in a blue long-sleeved gown bunched at her slim waist by a gold belt. Her dark, braided hair was wrapped around her head, forming a corded black turban. Antochlius caught a glimpse of calm, amused eyes and smelled the cloying perfume of malati flowers. Behind him, he could hear the sound of the roan's galloping hooves fading away.

The black-clad riders spurred their horses forward, but there was only one route to pursue her – and that led past him. He sat astride his stallion, sword in hand, defending the gap. Thorny bushes growing between the trees formed a barrier too thick for a horseman to pass through.

'My last stand,' he thought grimly. 'I hope the Brahmin rewards me well if I survive. Or at least gives me a decent funeral.'

The attackers were forced into funnel formation as they charged at Antochlius. The first one rushed forward, swinging his blade through the space where the Greek's head should have been. In a flash, he ducked and severed the attacker's head instead; the horse escaped with its owner's torso bobbing up and down on the bloody saddle. The next man collapsed, his sword falling from his hand, fingers clutching his throat where Antochlius's throw-knife had lodged itself, causing blood to gush out in great spasms. As he passed, Antochlius smelt his sweat, sour with panic. He cursed loudly. Death has different smells, he thought, recalling battles past, smelling again all the blood, shit and piss that had been part of his fighting life, and that of his father and his father before him.

After the fall of their two comrades, the remaining horsemen stopped a few yards away, watching Antochlius circling on his mount, protecting his position, his eyes never leaving them. The Greek felt the glare of the man in the chariot like the force of a small, furious star.

'It's an impasse,' Antochlius shouted. 'Go back the way you came, and none of you needs to die.'

The leader of the attackers, a tall man in black leather armour and a leather mask, laughed derisively. 'There are twelve of us left.' His voice dropped to a grim octave. 'You won't live long, Antochlius.'

Antochlius recognized the voice.

'Telemachus, the prime minister's bum boy?' He laughed mockingly. 'I can't imagine a Greek attacking a member of the king's bodyguard.'

Telemachus laughed unpleasantly. 'I'm a Greek, but I'm also a realist,' he said. 'I fight for gold, not just glory!'

'Telemachus, remember we are the sons of Greeks who came to India with the great Alexander,' Antochlius shouted. 'Our fathers have killed many brave men fearsome Persian horsemen, Mongols of the steppes and fierce mountain warriors of the Hindu Kush. They destroyed the war elephants and the battle chariots of

King Porus. We too are warriors, and serve the same king. Go back in peace, brother. Do not fight me.'

The small man in the chariot cackled loudly, sounding like a parrot squawking.

'You are not a Greek, Antochlius. You're the son of a Greek renegade and a Magadhan whore. When we capture the princess, finish off your army and drag your king through the mud to the execution ground in Kalingapatanam, we'll see how hot Magadha's blood is.'

Antochlius's face darkened. How did this man know so much about him and the girl?

'The Brahmin's agent is flabbergasted,' the small man sneered, his serpent bracelet blinking. 'Why don't you join us instead of fighting us? Tell us where the girl is headed and you'll never have to work again. A soldier's pay can't be much.' A heavy leather pouch flew through the air, clinking as it fell to the ground in front of Antochlius.

'There are a hundred silver coins inside, enough for you to live the rest of your life peacefully,' the man said. 'Enough to buy a farm, marry a wide-hipped woman and have many children. You'll be the king of your village.'

'I'm already married, so take your dirty money away,' Antochlius growled. 'You're not getting past me.'

He thought briefly about his family back in Pataliputra, the small wood-and-brick house in the middle of a neatly tended garden – his wife's pride – with a gravelled path leading to a yellow-painted door with a knocker in the shape of a minotaur.

'You are a bigger bull,' his wife would tease him

as they lay in bed watching the moon's lazy passage through their bedroom window. He thought of his little daughter, whom he would cradle in his arms when she cried. She would fall quiet only when he sang an old Greek song his father used to hum to him when he was a boy.

He thought of the Brahmin, who never left a wrong unavenged; a man with the blood of hundreds on his long-fingered hands. No, he couldn't betray the Brahmin for gold, or for anything else. He was tied to the coven of spies with bonds of blood. They would come for his wife and child if he betrayed them. He imagined the spymaster and the king's soldiers bursting into his little house and dragging his screaming wife away, tearing at her clothes and spreading her legs apart, laughing. He could see his daughter hoisted on a spear, its cruel shining end protruding from her little chest, her mouth open like a little rosebud. The blood, oh, the blood, and his wife's screams ... He shut his eyes tight and almost covered his ears with his palms... suddenly they felt so heavy... before he remembered where he was.

Even in his anguish, Antochlius understood that the Brahmin did what he did because he had to. There was no other way. Loyalty was rewarded with riches and betrayal with annihilation. The Brahmin defended his king with ruthless determination.

No, he couldn't take the fat man's gold. He had to fight and die here so that his wife and daughter could live.

At a command from Telemachus, a batch of horsemen

lunged at him. Antochlius drew his second sword. When they were almost upon him, he bent back on his saddle, stretching wide his arms diagonally. He heard the swoosh of their weapons pass above his head. His arms jerked with the impact of his blades slicing through the bone and flesh of his attackers. Their screams startled a flock of wild birds, which rose from the thickets in a panicked flutter of wingbeats. He felt the thick wetness of blood on his arm, and realized that an attacker's sword had nicked him. His horse was shiny with sweat and so was he.

He reined it in and glared at Telemachus.

'You want to die here,' his foe snarled. 'So be it.'

Antochlius reckoned the girl had had time enough to get back on the highway to Ujjain, where she would be safe. The pace at which the convoy had been moving, she would be able to meet up with them soon. Moreover, with war on his mind, Ashoka had deployed armed cavalry divisions to patrol the roads. She would be safe. Antochlius muttered a quick prayer and urged his horse forward, shouting Alexander's terrifying war cry: 'Alalalai!' His father had taught it to him as they trained with wooden sticks and later, swords, in the backyard of their house.

'Never forget who you are, my son,' Aeimnestus would say to him. 'Your mother may be from Pataliputra, but you are Alexander's spawn.'

He thought of his father standing guard in the palace, the protector of kings and a lion in battle. He wished he were here, fighting side by side with him. But Aeimnestus was far away.

Suddenly he was in the thick of battle, his sword scything through muscle and sinew as screams of rage and pain rang around him. He could feel his horse tiring under him, but he guided it along with his knees and calf muscles as he thrust and parried using both his swords, till one escaped his grip and was lost in the melee. His body was a bleeding mass of pain. Blood flowed from a cut in his forehead, almost blinding him. Amidst the savage cries of his enemies, he heard the little man encouraging his soldiers shrilly. Antochlius rushed towards the chariot with his sword held aloft, and the man fell back against the cushions in fright. Only the woman's eyes continued to regard him fearlessly. Antochlius gave his weary horse a powerful nudge with his ankles, pressing his thighs tight against its flanks; the Nissean drew upon its last reserve of strength and leaped over the chariot.

Antochlius slid down the right flank of his horse, his left foot firmly braced in its stirrup and left hand gripping his saddle horn as he swung his sword with his right hand, aiming for the little man's head. It missed, but he managed to grab the man's wrist. The serpent bracelet tore away in his hand. He felt his horse shudder as a spear entered its belly. His own head snapped back as he was thrown off its back by a giant force, a black-feathered arrow that had penetrated his throat. Antochlius felt an immense surge of relief that it was over. His wife and child were safe.

As he hit the ground, his body felt like one great wound. The pain was excruciating. He had fallen in the shade of an ancient oak, whose branches soared skywards, spreading away from the massive trunk like a benediction. He turned over with a grunt and clawed at the hard earth with bleeding fingernails to drag himself towards the tree. With each movement, pain squeezed his body with the fierceness of a betrayed lover.

'Take his head off.' He recognized Telemachus's voice. 'He has killed eight of our men and wounded three.'

'Stop.' The woman's voice rang out, clear as a bell. 'He fought like a true warrior and deserves to die like one.'

Antochlius had reached the shelter of the oak. He heaved himself up and lay back against its trunk. The woman's shadow fell over him. She knelt beside him and her soft palm caressed his bloody forehead. He remembered his wife's touch and almost wept.

'You fought well, Greek,' she said. 'It's a pity you didn't accept Lord Suma's offer. If Ashoka defeats Kalinga, it will be because of soldiers like you.'

He looked at her through a red mist and saw her gazing down with an expression of gentle regret. He grinned weakly.

'Where did the girl go?' she asked gently. 'Not that you'll tell us...'

'Find her!' the small man shouted.

'We will,' the woman said, with a promise in her melodious voice. 'But let me first reach Ujjain where my betrothed awaits.'

The man laughed. The woman stroked Antochlius's forehead. She sat down beside him and placed a small red flower on the ground.

'Who are you?' he whispered.

'I am Mur,' she said simply. She got up and walked towards the chariot.

In the depths of the forest, a lone wolf began to howl.

Brotherhood of Blood

The Brahmin and his assistant rode deeper into the forest, which lay before them like a primordial beast speckled with green, red, sienna and yellow. The sky formed a backdrop of silver slashed with purple, cloudless and calm. The sunlight felt cool, a reminder of winter's approach. An eagle drew lazy circles high above them, riding the thermals with untamed grace.

A relentless hunter who never gives up his prey, the Brahmin thought. Like a good spy.

As the two riders neared the forest, they felt a familiar tension grip them. Instinct, honed by years of surviving treachery, violence and death warned them to be ready to meet any danger.

The spymaster felt his vision expand and sharpen. He could identify small cracks in the barks of trees. He heard the whisper of a leaf falling and a branch creaking as a dreaming owl shifted on its perch. He saw in minute detail the soft, secret light illuminating every vein in every leaf. An ancient instinct took over accompanied by the salty taste of fear followed by a primitive power surging through every muscle and sinew. He recognized its might and fury and yielded to it as he had in battles before, when he had stood back to back with his liege, their swords cleaving through bodies, their forearms throbbing as they deflected blows with their shields, their knees thrusting into the groins of their attackers.

Savage memories flooded him, of the Battle of Taxila, before Ashoka became king. The fighting was fierce. The air thundered with war cries, and as the battle progressed, the terrible chorus of the dying and the wounded rose from the muddy, ravaged earth, churned into bloody slush by thousands of struggling feet. Many fallen soldiers were being crushed to death. The stench of blood, urine and shit was nauseating. In places, men fighting hand to hand desperately hacked at each other with swords and spears. Ashoka and he were protected by a cordon of bodyguards, whose numbers were dwindling slowly but steadily. Then suddenly a Magadhan cavalry charge broke the circle and fell upon the enemy, who retreated and then regrouped.

The Brahmin had never felt so afraid in his life.

Much later, he realized that it was this fear that gave him the strength to continue fighting even though every muscle of his body felt as if it was on fire. His face was covered with blood and gore, and he bled from a hundred cuts and wounds all over his body. He remembered Ashoka's face as a red grimy bloodstained mask through which his teeth gleamed like a demon's.

'You look like a ghost,' he told the Brahmin with a fierce grin before collapsing in a faint.

The fighting grew thick around them again.

Most of the horsemen defending them had been killed. The Brahmin hoisted Ashoka on his back and ran through the dead and dying, almost slipping on the bloody, slimy mud that sucked at his boots. He whistled for Garuda as he ran. The great warhorse rushed towards them, slashing at the enemy soldiers in its way with its cruel iron-tipped hooves. The Brahmin threw Ashoka on its back and leapt on the saddle behind him. Bodies were flung aside in various directions by the force of Garuda's massive shoulders as the great horse leapt forward, screaming in rage, ploughing through the mass of fighting men. Suddenly they were free and racing away from the battlefield.

The day was dying and Ashoka was losing blood. They rode hard and fast until Garuda grew weary. Then, just when it seemed that they could go no further, faint lights became visible on a rocky rise ahead, and a monastery came into view.

The Brahmin pushed his tiring horse up the winding narrow path that led to the gates. As he clattered into the courtyard, calling for help, three monks rushed out of the monastery. Their shaven heads gleamed in the light of torches on the sconces along the walls. Their yellow robes fluttered about them. They received Ashoka in their arms and swiftly took him indoors. For seven days and nights, the Brahmin sat by his side without sleep, watching monks come and go with medicines and poultices for Ashoka's wounds. They massaged him with warm oil mixed with the paste of healing herbs. They covered him with fresh earth, which they washed away with medicine-infused water. Every few hours, they applied a wet cloth to his forehead to bring the fever down. The room was kept dark and cool. The windows were covered with thick bamboo mats lined with black cloth to prevent sunlight from disturbing the patient's rest.

As the days passed, the Brahmin fell into a stupor, guarding his lord, eating just a little broth and a few pieces of cooked pork. He was aware of being watched but it did not bother him. Rather, he felt comforted, like a gentle but omnipotent guardian was watching over them both. On the seventh day, the Black Prince opened his eyes and let out a soft sigh. His gaze fell on the Brahmin. He laid a weak hand on his arm.

'Where am I? Am I a prisoner?' he asked.

'You are safe, my lord,' the Brahmin said. 'You are at the Tamralipti monastery and have been under the care of its good monks.'

He tried to rise from his seat and call out for assistance, but his legs buckled under him. His battle-weary body seemed light as a feather. As he fell and the darkness rose up to draw its soft, friendly mantle over him, strong arms caught him and laid him down gently on a straw-covered pallet. Briefly he glimpsed the face of a man. Below a wide, high forehead, thick smiling lips curved gently upwards. Large, heavily lidded eyes were luminous with soft light. Earlobes hung down almost to the shoulders, hair in a matted knot. The Brahmin caught the stranger's scent, a blend of sandalwood and lotus. He felt the pain leave his body, to be replaced by a heavy but pleasant sensation.

'Sleep, my son,' the man whispered. 'You have been very brave.'

When he woke, it was afternoon. Sunlight gilded the room. The windows were open, framing large squares of blue, cloudless sky. He heard bird song in the distance.

He smelt the fragrance of flowers. He turned his head and saw Ashoka sitting on a chair, gazing down at him thoughtfully.

'You saved my life,' the Black Prince said.

He bent down and stroked the Brahmin's forehead softly.

'I did what I had to do,' the Brahmin replied, his voice hoarse.

'I am grateful for what you did.'

The Brahmin laughed weakly. The effort made him cough.

'You are a prince and, one day, you will be king. Kings are never grateful.'

Ashoka nodded. 'Yes, kings are never in anyone's debt. But I am also a man. As a man, I am in your debt.'

'There is no need for that, my prince.'

'You slept for almost ten days. I watched over you like you did for me.'

The Brahmin sat up. He felt strength return to his body. He couldn't remember having felt so refreshed before. A physician monk came into the room, bearing a bowl of hot, thick soup. He placed it on a small wooden stool.

'This is suffused with medicinal herbs. Eat and you will feel strong,' he advised.

It tasted wonderful: thick, mixed with chicken cubes, peas and fresh carrots. He finished eating and got up.

'We have to leave now,' he said. 'My horse…'

The monk nodded.

'Your horses are fine, but they'll need the run back

home. They've been fed too well on oats, minced pork and lots of fresh grass, I fear.'

The Brahmin laughed. A young boy came in with a set of freshly pressed clothes. He laid them on a table and left without a word. Ashoka was already dressed. The Brahmin picked up a tunic and started to put it on. Then he stopped and turned towards the physician.

'But I was in the thick of the battle…' he stammered, confused.

He ran his hands over his body, which had been ravaged by a hundred cuts. The skin was smooth and supple, without the trace of a single scar. The monk smiled, his wise eyes crinkling in kind amusement. 'He caught you as you fell,' he said. 'Anyone he catches is forever safe.'

Ashoka eyed the monk keenly; his gaze was met with a calm smile.

He said, 'When I was sleeping, I had many dreams. In one of them, I felt someone was in the room, watching me. I couldn't see his face. His gaze was like a lamp. It healed me and made me feel safe.'

'Who was he?' the Brahmin asked.

'He is the master,' the monk replied.

'I know of no master,' replied Ashoka haughtily. 'One day I'll be the master of the world. It's my destiny.'

'My master owns nothing, except what we give him,' said the monk.

'What do you give him?'

'Our souls came the reply.'

'I would like to see him,' Ashoka demanded.

The monk shook his head regretfully. 'I'm afraid that's not possible, he left yesterday.'

'Where has he gone?'

'To Gaya.'

'If I ride fast, perhaps I can catch up with him. I wish to thank him. Which route did he take?'

'All roads lead to Gaya, so what difference does it make, my lord?' the monk answered. 'But he left a message for your companion.' He looked at the Brahmin. 'He said he will meet you again one day. Then will you know him and know yourself.' He turned back to Ashoka. 'Thus will he save you and your kingdom, my lord.'

'Why him? Why not me?' Ashoka demanded.

The monk shrugged.

'The master speaks in riddles,' he replied. 'Come, it's time for you to leave. Your horses are ready.'

Ashoka frowned at the Brahmin. Nobody had rejected his requests before. They strode down the monastery's wide stone stairs to a large courtyard with high walls. A group of monks was clustered together at the base of the steps like a farewell party. A young boy held the bridles of the horses. He smiled at the Brahmin and stroked Garuda's forehead. The Brahmin opened his mouth to shout a warning, then stopped as the great warhorse bent his head and nuzzled the boy's neck. Garuda did not usually like strangers and was known to kill anyone who came too close.

'This is not a place of cruelty but of mercy,' said the physician monk, reading his thoughts.

They were handed their weapons and cloaks.

'I will not forget your kindness, holy man,' Ashoka said, sliding his boots into the stirrups. His voice held a gentleness the Brahmin had not known he possessed. The monk nodded.

'The master wishes you a safe journey,' he said, bowing.

As they turned their horses around, they heard the sound of blows and the clash of heavy sticks. Loud fierce cries came from behind the building.

'Wait!' Ashoka called out at the retreating back of the monk. 'I thought this was a place of peace.'

The monk stopped, turned and bowed again.

'We are peaceful people. But there are warrior monks too. Soldiers sick of war, filled with guilt about the lives they took. They came looking for the master. One day, brigands attacked the monastery. The soldiers defended us. Most of them later became monks, but they are warriors still.'

He called out a name and a tall, lean man with a shaven head appeared. He was dressed in yellow robes and carried a long sword in his right hand. A bow was slung over his right shoulder, a quiver of arrows behind his left.

'Meet Angyo, one of our best fighters,' the monk said.

'An interesting name, what does it mean?' Ashoka asked.

'It means peacemaker.'

'I can see how he makes peace,' the Brahmin said dryly, eyeing the sword.

'I thought your master preaches peace,' Ashoka said.

'True. And it has to be kept. All conflicts are the same. One attacks and the other defends.'

'Isn't this principle contrary to your beliefs?'

'When you kill to defend the innocent, you are doing the right thing. When you attack evil, you fight for the light.'

'But who decides what is innocent or evil?' asked Ashoka.

'Your true soul. Every person in this world is constantly at war, with themselves the most. The day you win over yourself, you'll become a warrior of the light.'

'A bunch of monk talk which means nothing to me,' Ashoka sneered. He gave a mock bow and swung his warhorse's head towards the plains below. The Brahmin did the same. Out of habit, both drew their weapons to check their condition. Blue steel shone in the sun, the blades honed to an edge that could cut a feather in half.

Suddenly a warning cry sounded and the high walls of the monastery were lined with bowmen. A troop of armed monks swarmed into the courtyard from the back. The physician held up his hand. The archers lowered their bows and the fighters stopped advancing.

Ashoka laughed uneasily.

'I almost thought you had us there,' he barked.

The monks did their work well, both in war and in peace.

The memory of hissing steel woke the Brahmin from his reverie. They had reached the hem of the forest. He noticed Hao's curious gaze. His sword was in his hand. He didn't remember having drawn it.

'You were far away, though you were riding so close,' Hao said. 'It's the war, isn't it? Old ones and those ahead.'

The Brahmin shrugged.

The two spies entered the forest path, which had become narrow and dark as the shadows of trees closed in. Sunlight filtered through the endless canopy above, giving the atmosphere an unearthly green glow. A leopard roared somewhere deep in the forest. A group of monkeys hurried through the trees above, chattering wildly and causing the horses to become skittish.

The Brahmin leaned forward and whispered soothing words in Garuda's ear, his hand gripping his sword tightly. As they penetrated deeper into the forest, the shadows grew darker. Moss blanketed the bark of great, venerable trees, covering them with a thick green gloss. Bright flowers bloomed on vines. Creepers were wound around tree trunks. A python dozed on a low branch.

'Never mind him, he has eaten well,' said the Brahmin, pointing at the snake's swollen middle.

With a loud flutter of wings, a flock of wood pigeons clattered out from the dense foliage. The trees were gigantic, with imposing black trunks. At a curve ahead, they grew thickly together, almost obscuring the narrow clearing. On their left stood a cluster of large boulders. An oval-shaped clearing lay ahead.

'A perfect spot for an ambush,' Hao remarked.

They stopped.

'Look at the ground there,' the Brahmin pointed. He jerked his thumb back and signalled to Hao. She walked her horse towards a large boulder and disappeared from his view. The Brahmin's knees tightened on Garuda's flanks and the horse tensed its muscles, ready to leap. The

Brahmin whistled sharply and Garuda charged around the bend, straight into the clearing. Hao's horse swung out from behind the boulder. But the place was empty.

The two spies dismounted and inspected the scene of battle. Hooves and boot heels had dug up the earth. The wheels of a chariot had scoured the ground. Pieces of bloody garments were scattered all around and the ground was scoured where bodies appeared to have been dragged away. The Brahmin peered through the trees and saw fresh mounds of earth – hastily dug graves. Hao pointed to a long trail of blood. It led to an oak tree beyond the clearing under which lay a man. His face was a mask of dried blood. There were deep gashes on his chest and shoulders. A black-fletched arrow had penetrated his throat, right below the jaw. He raised his head and looked at the Brahmin with dull, glazed eyes. It was Antochlius.

The spymaster knelt beside his dying spy. Hao pulled a flask of water out of her saddlebag and handed it to the Brahmin. He raised Antochlius gently, parted his lips and tipped its contents into his mouth.

'Who did this to you?' he asked gently.

'The princess,' Antochlius whispered with great difficulty. 'She is safe.'

He gasped. His eyelids fluttered for a moment. Then his eyes opened wide, full of intelligence and clarity.

'I did it for you, master, I did my best. The Blood Flower...' he said in a clear, firm voice, then he fell back and died. His right hand lay outstretched on the ground, the fist closed tight. Hao prised the fingers open and held up a bracelet shaped like a serpent, smudged with blood.

The Brahmin's face darkened. He remembered where he had last seen one like it. He vowed to make Kalinga pay. It was no longer a game of spies. This one was personal.

Stranger's Strategem

They buried Antochlius under the old oak tree and rode on. It took them two more days to reach the outskirts of Ujjain. Four days were left for Ashoka's deadline to be over.

A soft winter mist hovered over the land as the exhausted Brahmin and Hao passed through several small towns and villages. They crossed marketplaces full of vegetable vendors trying to out-yell each other like raucous ravens and fat shopkeepers wrapped in thick woollen shawls, squatting crosslegged in front of huge sacks of grain, pulses and jaggery. The mansions of noblemen and rich merchants they passed were built on tall wooden platforms, with grey Chunar sandstone pillars supporting painted, multicoloured roofs. Only their tops were visible because the houses stood in the middle of large orchards with high brick walls. The scent of mangoes, guavas and pomegranates perfumed the air.

The two riders stopped at an inn, which claimed to serve the 'best capon curry in Magadha.' Capons, or roosters castrated to preserve the tenderness of their flesh, were a byproduct of Alexander's Greek invasion.

They invited surprised glances when they entered. The Brahmin imagined how he must appear to strangers: a tall, dark warrior with a shaven head, wearing a travel-stained capote, muddy boots, and a sword hanging low from a war belt slung across powerful shoulders. Hao got even more curious looks as she threw off her dusty, hooded cape, revealing thick black hair and ivory skin. Her slanting eyes were dark and watchful. The ivory-handled daggers in her belt also attracted attention.

The Brahmin heard her swift intake of breath and followed the direction of her gaze to a slim, fair woman sitting alone at a table in the corner. At the table next to her was a group of burly men playing dice and eating salted rice dumplings from copper plates. One of them, almost big enough to be called a giant, his face sulky and unshaven, seemed to be their leader. The woman had an oval face and long, dark hair worn in thick braids around her head, like a corded turban. She was dressed in a loose blue long-sleeved gown bunched below her breasts. A golden girdle accentuated the slimness of her waist. The glass bangles on her hand tinkled when she raised her glass of wine to her mouth. Her lower lip was red, full and sensual. Her large, dark kohl-rimmed eyes curved up slightly, giving her a slightly Oriental cast like Hao's, but less pronounced. They regarded the visitors with interest. Hao turned away muttering a curse, her mouth set in a grim line.

'Know her?' the Brahmin asked.

'The likes of these soft creatures belong either to a brothel or a harem. The former, most likely. I do not belong to either,' she snapped.

The spymaster nodded a greeting at the woman. Hao glared at her, her right hand on the hilt of her dagger. The woman threw her a dimpled smile. The giant noticed the exchange. His hand went to the battle-axe tucked into his leather belt. She leaned across and laid a hand on his arm, her sleeve riding up for a moment to reveal a thin snake-shaped gold bracelet with tasseled red braids. With a growl, he spat on the mud floor and sat down. A thick blob of phlegm landed inches away from the Brahmin's dusty boots.

'I apologise for my bodyguard's rudeness,' the woman said in a low musical voice, placing her wine glass on the table. 'He gets jealous sometimes.'

The spymaster shrugged, his face impassive though he had recognized the bracelet on the woman's arm as one Kalingan envoys wore. A diplomat? A spy? He would have to be careful. 'I meet all sorts on my travels,' he replied in a level voice. 'Each to his own.'

The woman withdrew her hand from the man's thick forearm and pulled down her sleeve.

'I would have asked you to join me,' she said, 'but my bodyguards are reluctant to let strangers come near me. You see, the road is dangerous and infested with brigands and cut-throats. A helpless woman like me needs protection.'

The Brahmin laughed. 'Now I am offended,' he said.

'Oh no!' Her hand flew to her soft mouth in false dismay. 'I didn't mean to accuse you of being robbers.'

'Where are you bound, my lady?' the spymaster asked, infusing warmth into his voice he did not feel. Her eyes widened with mock innocence.

'Why, to Ujjain, of course, like you.'

'Like us? How do you know that?' Hao interjected sharply.

'Isn't this the highway to the city?' the woman retorted with a smile.

The spymaster's instincts were on full alert. Careful, he told himself.

'You have us there,' he said, shrugging off his cloak and flinging it over a chair at the next table. Hao did the same, frowning darkly.

'You look like warriors,' the woman continued, ignoring Hao's look. 'Or court officials, perhaps.'

'It's odd for a woman like you, beautiful and obviously wealthy, to travel with these…' Hao interrupted with a contemptuous wave of her hand, indicating the men at the table. The woman frowned.

'They are good men who would kill for me,' she said. Her voice was cold. 'I always choose the best fighters to accompany me when I travel.'

'They would guard anyone who pays them enough gold, sister,' Hao retorted. 'Until the next one pays them more to kill.'

'Oh, sisters are we, now? I don't think so,' the woman said snootily, wrinkling her nose at Hao's muddy cape and dust-darkened face and picking up her glass.

Hao's face flushed deep red. 'I agree. I don't have a sister who is some fat lord's whore,' she snapped.

The Brahmin was mildly irritated with Hao for picking a fight with this comely stranger for no apparent reason. She didn't usually do that. He wondered why. But he didn't miss the slight movement of the woman's knee against her bodyguard's leg. With a savage grunt, the brute leaped over the table, smacking one hand down on its wooden surface while pulling out his axe with the other, ready to strike even before he landed on the floor. With a speed that was almost supernatural, Hao moved sideways and came up behind him, her dagger pressed against his spine.

The Brahmin shook his head. 'I wouldn't do anything stupid if I were you,' he warned.

Silence froze the room. Nobody moved. The woman's hand paused mid-air, her wine glass half raised towards her red mouth, her eyebrows raised in silent appreciation. Her glistening lips were parted, her eyes wide and large, shining with bloodlust. Her men sat still, as if the slightest movement could change the situation. Then she placed her glass carefully on the table, clapped and let out a musical peal of laughter.

'Step back, Pippalli,' she told her henchman. 'Drop your axe.'

The bodyguard obeyed reluctantly. With a grunt, he stepped back and glared at Hao, eyes filled with hate.

'Another time, slant eyes,' he growled. He picked up the axe and returned to his seat.

The woman rose from her seat and slapped the man. His head snapped back and, for a moment, murder flashed in his eyes. Ignoring him, she walked over to the visitors and held out her hand. The Brahmin kissed it lightly.

'I am Mur,' she murmured. 'I am sorry about Pippalli's conduct. He should know better than to speak like that to a woman. Any woman. He will be duly punished. But I am delighted to make your acquaintance. Now can I have my hand back?'

The Brahmin caressed her wrist gently. As she withdrew her hand, her bracelet glinted briefly.

'That's an interesting ornament, unlike any other I've seen,' he observed pleasantly. 'Its design is so simple, yet beautiful. May I see it?'

Mur pouted and shook her head, hand held behind her back. 'It's a gift from my fiancé. He made me promise never to take it off. And that's an interesting ring on your finger, by the way. It looks very important.'

'It's just a ring,' the Brahmin shrugged.

Why was she lying about her bracelet? She could have mentioned she was a diplomat traveling to Ujjain, probably to the embassy there. She had to be a spy. The Brahmin realised a deadly game of wits had begun between him and the beautiful spy. He wondered about her mission. Whatever it was, he was sure it would reach its climax in Ujjain, where the queen was. Mur walked across to his table.

'May I join you?' She sat down beside Hao without waiting for an answer. Hao grimaced and edged away.

The Brahmin ordered well-cooked capon in mustard gravy, spiced with fried shallots, a bowl of boiled vegetables and roasted wheat cakes. Hao asked for a dish of kodrava rice seasoned with spring onions, peas and spicy goat meat along with a pot of rice wine. Mur raised her delicately plucked eyebrows.

'You are hungry, aren't you, sister?' she asked Hao with a trace of smiling sarcasm.

'Long ride,' Hao replied brusquely, refusing to rise to the bait.

When the innkeeper came in with the food, Mur nodded to him in a familiar fashion.

'Ah Karaka, I hope you'll look after our friends as well as you look after me.'

The man's furtive eyes went to the Brahmin and his aide. He smiled crookedly.

'You haven't told me where you are going,' Mur said, taking a sliced cucumber from the Brahmin's bowl and nibbling it delicately.

'Ujjain,' he replied.

'Official business, I suppose,' she said.

'You said you are on your way to Ujjain, too, *sister*. Would it be rude to ask why?' Hao asked with a sneer in her voice.

'My fiancé, Aryaputra Devavarman, lives there,' came the reply. 'He is the viceroy of Ujjain.'

The Brahmin stroked his chin thoughtfully. A Kalingan spy engaged to a prince of Magadha? It was bad news for the kingdom.

'Isn't Devavarman a nephew of Amatya Rudradaman?' the Brahmin asked.

Amatyas were powerful judicial and administrative officials in Magadha who monitored the affairs of the kingdom and had direct access to the monarch. Aryaputras, who were of royal lineage, governed the provinces. Mur's eyes narrowed.

'Do you know him?' she asked.

'Not really,' replied the Brahmin. 'I've met him a few times at court.'

Devavarman was a weak-chinned young man running

to fat, spoilt and arrogant, who spent most of his time gambling, whoring and drinking. Though he was an Aryaputra, the actual administration was done by efficient pradeshikas in charge of the districts. The Brahmin knew this because two of them were his spies.

He glanced at Mur, who met his eyes with a wide, innocent gaze. If one of Lord Suma's spies had penetrated the Magadhan administrative service, the situation was more serious than he had thought.

Lord Suma held the advantage, for now.

It would not be difficult for a beautiful and seductive woman like Mur to get information from Pataliputra, using Devavarman's connection with his powerful uncle.

The Brahmin cursed his spies in Ujjain. Why hadn't they informed him of this dubious allegiance? And how did a Kalingan spy, and that too one so beautiful, manage to skip the attention of his informers? Mur interrupted his thoughts by filling his plate with food, ignoring Hao altogether.

'You must be hungry,' she said softly.

Hao grunted dismissively and reached for the bowl of rice.

The Brahmin shook his head, amused.

He hadn't realized how tired and hungry he was until he began to eat. The landlord came out of the kitchen with a jar of wine. The spymaster was aware of Mur's men watching him.

Suddenly he didn't want to go to Ujjain. He didn't want to meet the queen. He didn't want to find the murderer of the concubine. He didn't want to run his vast network of spies, assassins and vishakanyas – beautiful young seductresses who had been fed small, prescribed potions of poison as little girls, so that when they grew to maturity, their fluids proved deadly for the men they were ordered to entrap and kill. The Brahmin simply wanted to rest.

He felt fatigue cover him like a heavy mantle, followed by a languor so deep that he felt he was in a dream. In it, he saw Hao asleep. Her cheek rested on the wooden table, upon which her meal sat unfinished. He saw four burly men rise from their bench and move towards them. He saw Mur glide away like a fairy disappearing into the forest mist. As she left, something floated down from the folds of her gown, something familiar. But his senses felt too heavy to recall where he had seen something like it. The men were coming closer, weapons drawn. The spymaster knew he had been drugged or poisoned, and that his life was over. He gave a deep sigh, half full of gratitude because he didn't have to live in a world of lies anymore, not trusting anyone completely, not even Hao. He sighed because he was defeated, his mission unfinished. Then, through the muslin net of descending darkness, he heard the door of the inn crash open, and saw a tall cloaked figure sweep in with a raised sword, its blade shining like the vengeance of god, before the eternal night descended on him.

A Warrior Interferes

'So, this is hell,' the Brahmin thought.

His throat was parched as though the tender skin inside had been rubbed away with sandpaper. His limbs felt as if iron chains bound them. He was lying motionless on a straw mattress in a dimly lit room. Hao snored close by.

'This can't be heaven surely.' The Brahmin thought of all the blood that stained his hands from his efforts to keep the kingdom and his king safe.

'If it's not hell, then it must be purgatory, for my throat is on fire and all my bones seem to be broken. But I don't see any demons yet,' he mused.

The door opened and a caped figure walked in with a lantern. The Brahmin groaned. So he was in hell after all. Here was a monster who had come to punish him for all the men and women he had destroyed in Ashoka's name.

The visitor knelt beside the Brahmin and raised his light.

'You've slept for a long time, my friend.' The voice was soft and familiar, but the Brahmin couldn't place it. He tried to get up. The stranger pushed him slowly back on the mattress and said, 'Your wine was poisoned with the pulp of amanita mushrooms. Luckily for you, I found some belladonna in the back garden.'

Belladonna was the best antidote for the lethal mushrooms. Killing one poison with another. Sounds like espionage, the Brahmin mused grimly.

'You're in the loft of the same inn where you almost died,' the man said. 'After a little gentle persuasion, the innkeeper allowed me to take you both up to the loft and make you comfortable, then kindly gave me access to his little herbarium. I wouldn't have guessed our man was such a good herbalist and gardener.'

'Who are you?' the Brahmin asked.

'I...' The stranger froze in mid-sentence. His face tightened and he pulled his broad shoulders back. Hao held a dagger to his throat. Her other hand was encircled around his neck. The Brahmin could never stop being surprised at her silent speed: she had been asleep when the man came in.

'Answer the question, stranger,' the Viet woman hissed.

'Obviously, your dose of poison wasn't as strong as your friend's,' the man said with mild regret and choked as she tightened her hold on his neck.

'Who are you?' she snapped.

'I'm from Tamralipti,' he croaked as her blade pressed against his throat.

The Brahmin shook his head. She stepped back. The stranger massaged his neck and smiled ruefully.

'You have a peculiar way of thanking those who save your lives,' he said.

'You don't recognize me?' He turned to the Brahmin, rubbing his neck vigorously.

Recognition flooded the spymaster, of a tall, lean monk with a sword in his hand and a bow slung over his shoulders.

'Angyo! How is it that you are here?'

The monk smiled. 'I've been with you ever since you left Pataliputra,' he answered.

'You are the rider who was following us!' exclaimed Hao.

He nodded.

'Why?' the Brahmin asked.

'To ensure no harm befell you.'

'We're quite capable of looking after ourselves,' Hao said haughtily.

'I noticed,' Angyo said drily.

'Why are the monks of Tamralipti interested in protecting us?' asked the Brahmin.

'Let's say we have our own interests,' Angyo answered with an inscrutable smile.

Damn these monks, they have to turn everything into a riddle, the Brahmin thought.

In the lantern's buttery light, Angyo looked like a mysterious, benevolent angel. The small square glass window of the loft's roof was beginning to lighten with the morning's tentative touch. The last song of a nightingale trilled with fading melody, as if no lovers had dallied in its garden, alive to the soft music of the night. Angyo searched the pockets of his riding robe and took out two vials. He held them out.

'Here, drink this. It will banish the remaining effects of the poison and refresh you.'

He was right.

As they descended the steep narrow stairs from the loft, the spymaster marvelled at their rescuer's strength. Carrying two people up must have required enormous effort.

Downstairs, the landlord was slumped over a table, his face slack, mouth open, and head askew where it had been nearly severed from the torso. A short, wicked looking dagger lay at his feet. The Brahmin looked questioningly at Angyo, who said, 'I merely asked him about you. He shouldn't have pulled a knife on me.'

'I thought you people believed in non-violence,' the Brahmin pointed out.

'We do. But sadly, others don't,' Angyo replied.

He went up to the corpse and pulled Ashoka's lion ring off the index finger. He tossed it to the Brahmin.

'Your attackers didn't steal it,' Angyo observed. 'The ring would have been recognized had they tried to sell it. These were no ordinary robbers.'

The Brahmin wasn't listening. He walked across to Mur's table and picked up something from the floor. He remembered his dream. The folds of her cloak opening. Something floating down. His face was sombre as he slipped it into his pocket.

They stepped outside. It had rained the night before. The brickyard was wet and muddy. The Brahmin remembered dreaming about the rain – a troubled, drugged dream. In it, rain slashed at the windows and doors of the inn, beating furiously on the stone walls. Antochlius was walking through the pelting water, holding his severed head in his hands. He held it out to the Brahmin.

'The princess,' his dead lips whispered.

'One of my best spies was killed,' the spymaster told Angyo. 'He was ambushed.'

'I know,' the monk admitted. 'I saw it.'

'Why didn't you intervene?' Hao asked angrily.

Angyo spread his sinewy hands. 'I don't have the power or the permission to interfere with fate, as the Buddha has taught us. I don't act until my master tells me to,' he said.

'Then why did you save us? Wasn't that interfering with fate?' the Brahmin asked.

'I didn't interfere. I was ordered to keep you safe. Now our fates are entwined.'

'Who ordered you?'

'Too many questions, so few answers,' Angyo said cryptically. The spymaster realized it was useless to inquire further. Instead, he asked, 'Who killed Antochlius? Did you see them?'

'I was on my way to the inn where I guessed you would halt for the night. Antochlius was on his way to Pataliputra in the company of a girl. I couldn't see her face because they were far away.'

'What happened to her?'

'She escaped. I saw her riding away in the direction of Ujjain.'

'Were you protecting us or spying on us?' demanded Hao.

'If I don't spy on you, how will I protect you? Who knows who or what might suddenly leap out of the dark?' Angyo said, smiling.

He pointed at the sullen sky, heavy with great black rainclouds. A feeble sun was trying to spin some copper into them, but was losing the fight.

'War is looming over the land, like those clouds,' Angyo said sombrely. 'Where there is war, there is intrigue. These are troubled times, my friend.'

He clapped the spymaster on the back with a rough, calloused hand. It was the hand of a warrior.

'Come, let's find our rides,' he said, striding towards the back of the inn.

Their horses were stabled in a barn in the company of two cows, an old bull and a few wet chickens cowering under the straw. Garuda whinnied with pleasure on seeing his master. Hao put her arms around her horse, and it rubbed her neck with its wet nose. Angyo's horse was stabled beside Garuda, an imposing Akhal Teke stallion from the steppes. Its long ears flicked as it turned hooded, almond-shaped eyes towards Angyo and gave a soft, glad whimper.

'No wonder you carry the Scythian bow,' the Brahmin said, pointing at Angyo's curved weapon.

The archers of the steppes were partial to the bow, which allowed them to shoot backwards over the rumps of their mounts. They were perfect weapons for cavalry men.

As they rode out into the grim morning on the winding road to Ujjain, the Brahmin asked Angyo for more details on Antochlius's death. When he finished, the Brahmin bowed his head, as if deep in prayer. Hao knew better. The master was plotting revenge. He looked up at Angyo and said, 'He was my man. A good man. A brave man. And you let him die.'

Angyo smiled regretfully. 'But he was not my man,' he replied.

The Brahmin let out a long breath and nodded. 'Now what?' he asked.

'You ride on to Ujjain,' said the monk.

'Are you coming with us?' Hao asked.

'Who knows?' Angyo gave an ironic salute and turned away, spurring his horse towards the forest, away from them and Ujjain.

'A cruel man with compassion,' Hao remarked. 'That's a strange combination.'

'A disciplined man,' said the Brahmin.

He gave a low whistle and slapped Garuda's flanks. The great stallion neighed loudly and picked up its stride. Behind him, Hao rode crouched low on her saddle, bent over the sleek, powerful neck of her black beast as they raced towards where Asandhimitra and murder awaited them.

The Queen's Illusion

Queen Asandhimitra, or Agramahisis as the chief queen was referred to, was slight of build, with intelligent, lustrous eyes, which could become sharp and penetrating on occasion. She wore her long black hair drawn back and tied at the nape of her neck, which was encircled by a simple gold chain from which hung a ruby lion pendant set in gold. Around her wrist was a gold bracelet, also with Ashoka's lion engraved in it. The king had given it to her on their wedding day and she had promised never to take it off.

The Brahmin and Hao were in the receiving room of her private chamber.

'I am glad to see you, spymaster,' she said in a low, flute-like voice from her cushioned chair by the fire that burned in a large carved stone hearth, which dominated the room. 'You do not kneel in front of my husband, so why this charade in front of me?'

'I'm afraid for my neck, Your Majesty. If I bow my head before the king, he might suddenly get the urge to chop it off. You know how temperamental he can be.'

Asandhimitra gave a loud peal of laughter as she bade them rise. The Brahmin could never stop marvelling at the girlishness of the most powerful woman in the kingdom. But she was nobody's fool.

'Do you bring me a message from my king?' she demanded.

'I am in search of a murderer, my lady. The murder of his concubine has disturbed the king greatly. He feels that if the heavily guarded women in his harem can be killed, then no one is free from harm. He is worried for your safety, Your Majesty.'

The queen nodded thoughtfully and said, 'Yes, I heard about the murder. The poor girl.' The Brahmin sensed tightly controlled unease beneath her even manner, concern that extended beyond the tragic death of a concubine. Asandhimitra was Ashoka's most beloved wife, but not his first. While he was the viceroy of Ujjain, he had married a young woman called Devi, the daughter of a local merchant. The people of Ujjain said she was related to Sakyamuni Buddha. The first few years of their marriage were harmonious. Ashoka was besotted with his new wife and they had two children, Mahendra and Sanghamitra. For years, Devi tried to persuade Ashoka to stop waging war and become a Buddhist, but failed. When he left for Pataliputra with an army to capture the throne, his family did not accompany him.

As if she could read his mind, Asandhimitra said sadly, 'Men like blood and death, while we women fear it. War is a widow-maker. If anyone else were to say it, they would be executed for treason, but if something were to happen to my beloved husband in the war…' She did not complete the sentence.

'Do not be afraid, Your Majesty. The king knows how to take care of himself. Besides, I am always with him, both in peace and war.'

'It's not Ashoka but the kingdom I am worried about.

If any harm befalls him, Magadha will be left heirless. I want you to do something for me, Brahmin. No, I command you.'

The spymaster bowed in obeisance.

'I have not been able to give my husband any children. You must find Devi, and ask her to go to Pataliputra with Mahendra and Sanghamitra. If Ashoka falls, I will crown Mahendra king.'

Asandhimitra's eyes brimmed with tears.

'As you wish, Your Majesty.'

He made a mental note to send for the prince.

'Enough of this grim talk.' Asandhimitra rose, her hand gripping his forearm. 'Your task here is to find the killer.'

'Your Majesty, the king has given me seven days to find him, and three days are already over. It's my neck on the block or the killer's. And I love my neck,' the Brahmin said.

'I am sure four days are enough for you to capture a killer. But for now, murder can wait, for I have to go to the Royal Hall. Come with me,' she commanded.

Something in her voice worried him A slight, trembling shadow of doubt.

Or was it fear?

The Brahmin and Hao followed the queen to a great hall whose polished wooden walls were festooned with costly rugs and muslin hangings depicting scenes of hunts, lovers locked in embrace and peacocks dancing in gardens. On a gilded platform in the centre stood two golden thrones supported by ivory statues of four lions each. When Ashoka visited Ujjain, Asandhimitra sat beside him and held court here. Together, they disposed of pleas and complaints, listening to details of taxes collected, conferring with judges and ministers, and passing judgment on criminals and those accused of treason. The throne was surrounded by a rectangle of white marble pillars, covered with fine carvings. The air smelt of jasmine; the pillars were hollow from the inside, and the sculptors had bored tiny, almost invisible holes in each one, so fresh flowers could be placed in them every morning. The room was cool in summer and warm in winter, thanks to the complex warren of channels that ran through the walls and under the polished floors. These were connected to great vats, which were heated in winter and cooled with snow brought from the northern mountains in summer.

As the Brahmin entered the Royal Hall behind the queen, his chest swelled with emotion as he observed the grace and dignity with which she carried herself. He loved this woman and would gladly die for her, if the occasion ever rose.

The sound of gongs and conches announced her arrival. Sword hilts thundered on iron shields and spear shafts thudded on the floor in unison, silencing the chatter in the hall. Asandhimitra took her seat. The Brahmin and Hao took position on either side of her. Beneath them, ringing the platform, the royal guard stood in rigid formation – young, muscular soldiers, grizzled Greek fighters, other veterans of Bindusara's campaigns, swordsmen and spear-carriers of the southern hills. He recognized many of them, for some were part of the queen's entourage and travelled with her to various parts of the kingdom. One of them, a powerful looking old warrior, looked familiar, but try as he might, the Brahmin couldn't place him. Asandhimitra was not a queen who preferred to luxuriate in the palace, gossiping with her ladies and organizing dances and feasts to amuse the king. She visited the big cities and important towns of the kingdom and conferred with officials to see for herself how matters stood. Often she held court, under a tree in a village square or in one of the palaces in a distant city. Ashoka paid attention to her advice, for he knew her mind was keener than that of most of his ministers.

Now, in the Royal Hall, the audience had risen from their seats when the queen entered. She ordered them to be seated.

It was then the Brahmin heard Hao's quick intake of breath. Asandhimitra heard it too, but gave no sign. In the middle of the first row of guests sat Mur and Lord Suma. Mur was in a silver silk gown which showed off her curves to best effect. She wore a loop of silver chains around her neck. Silver rings set with diamonds decorated her fingers. Silver earrings, each one inlaid with a large blue sapphire, dangled from her shell-like ears. When she shifted in her seat, she gave the illusion of having been painted with a cold blue fire. Next to her was a weak-chinned young man in a canary-yellow shirt, which did not conceal the bulge of his expanding belly. He wore bejewelled sandals and gold rings on his fat fingers. On his vacuous face, a pair of red, sensuous lips pouted between fat cheeks. His eyes looked glazed, as if he had imbibed some powerful drug. The Brahmin recognized him as Devavarman, the viceroy engaged to Mur.

'A dandy,' he thought. 'A dandy with a weak brain and a powerful uncle.'

He noticed the snake bracelet glittering on Suma's wrist, shiny and new. Suma rose and bowed low before the queen.

'Your Majesty, may I present my niece, Mur?' he said unctuously. 'It is a matter of pride that the great kingdoms of Magadha and Kalinga will be united in peace.'

Mur rose and bowed modestly.

'How so, Lord Suma?' Asandhimitra asked.

'She is to wed me.' The viceroy got up, panting a little at the effort.

The queen raised her finely drawn eyebrows.

'When?'

'On the tenth day of the tenth month of this year. My astrologers said it is the most auspicious day for my wedding.'

'We were not aware of this, Devavarman,' Asandhimitra said, a steely timbre entering her voice. 'Have you taken the king's permission to wed, Devavarman?'

The viceroy began to sweat. Panic flashed in his eyes. He kept pulling rings off his fingers and pushing them back. Mur laid a comforting hand on his arm.

'Perhaps Uncle was rather hasty in announcing it, Your Majesty,' she murmured. 'We have already sent a messenger to Pataliputra seeking the king's approval.'

'I know Kalinga has a boy-king who cannot change his own clothes,' Asandhimitra's voice rang with contempt. 'Here, my lord Ashoka commands everything, life and death, weddings and funerals.'

She turned fiercely towards Devavarman. 'Aryaputra, were you not aware of the law before you bleated out your wedding plans to me, your queen?' she demanded. 'Or are you so besotted that you forgot you are the viceroy?'

Devavarman prostrated himself before her. The Brahmin noticed the contempt in Mur's eyes and the rage, kept under check, behind Suma's smile.

'I suggest you travel to Pataliputra immediately to ask the king for mercy. You have done something stupid by deciding to marry a Kalingan girl, however beautiful, without your king's leave.'

She turned to Suma. 'You should accompany them, ambassador. It will take the best of your diplomatic skills to avert a catastrophe.'

'But... Your Majesty...' Suma spluttered.

Asandhimitra held up a hand. Devavarman cringed. He said nervously, 'Your Majesty, not even a week has passed since I returned from a council with the king. He had summoned all the four viceroys of the kingdom to discuss some confidential matters.'

'Why did you not ask him for permission to marry Mur then? Go back to him, Devavarman, and fall at his feet and beg for mercy. And make sure you return with your head on your shoulders. After all, the girl cannot marry a headless man,' Asandhimitra snapped.

Mur's face was red. In the effort to control herself, her nails dug into her palm.

'And see me tonight before you go,' Asandhimitra commanded. 'I have much to say to you.'

Devavarman curtsied, almost sobbing with fear, and left the hall in a fluster.

It was only then that Suma glanced at the Brahmin, his eyes widening in mock surprise.

'I am sorry I did not notice you before,' he said.

Unless he was blind in one eye, he could not have missed the Brahmin standing next to the queen. The spymaster decided to let Suma have his way.

'Lord Suma,' he said in acknowledgment.

'I am so glad to see you again after our meeting in the king's chamber in Pataliputra,' Suma continued. 'We have much to discuss, especially about your visit to my country.'

'I have to settle some matters first,' the Brahmin said.

The ambassador turned to Asandhimitra, his eyes sad.

What an excellent actor, the spymaster thought.

'I have something to discuss with you, Your Majesty. Something vital to both our kingdoms. I hear some disturbing rumours…' Suma began.

She cut him short.

'Rumours? We do not look kindly upon bazaar gossip. Neither should you, in my presence.'

Suma cleared his throat meaningfully.

'May we confer in private?' he asked.

'I do not confer in private with anyone except the king. On other occasions, my spymaster remains with me.'

'So be it, Your Majesty. I wished to convey my concern about the unfortunate death of the royal concubine in Pataliputra. I believe the killer is yet to be found. Can Kalinga be of any assistance? You left Pataliputra unexpectedly. The murder must have upset you.'

Asandhimitra closed her eyes briefly and sighed, resting her chin lightly on a beringed finger. A slim, square-shaped gold bangle gleamed on her slender wrist. The ornament, made of gold brought from the Hatti mines from the deep South bore a miniature medallion embossed with a Buddha head. It was part of the spoils of war that Ashoka had brought home after suppressing a revolt in Taxila. The city was associated with the Chinese traveller Fa-Hien, who gave it the name 'Cut off Head' since a Jataka legend said Taxila was where the Buddha in his previous birth as Chandaprabha had removed his own head to feed a hungry lion. Asandhimitra loved the bangle so much that she vowed to Ashoka that it would be removed from her hand only after her death. Now, she toyed with the Buddha head on the bangle, and fixed Suma with a cool, speculative glance,

'What murder?' she asked.

The diplomat was flustered. Then he rallied, a sympathetic expression on his face.

'I heard a concubine was murdered in Pataliputra,' he said.

'Really? None of them was missing when we left. Then who was it?'

'I only have a vague description of her, Your Majesty. But I believe she had a birthmark resembling a crescent moon on her left hand.'

'How poetic.' The queen gave a sarcastic laugh. 'I never knew spies could be poetic.'

Suma drew himself up haughtily.

'I am not a spy, Your Majesty. I am a representative of the king of Kalinga. But as a diplomat, I hear much gossip. I was told a girl had been kidnapped from the harem and murdered. And that her body was burned afterwards.'

'Many girls die in Pataliputra. What does it have to do with the harem?' Asandhimitra snapped.

She summoned one of her ladies-in-waiting and murmured an instruction. The woman left the hall and returned shortly with a heavily veiled girl dressed in a green filigreed velvet gown that covered almost her entire form.

'Don't be afraid, child, hold out your right hand,' Asandhimitra told her gently.

Glass bangles tinkled on her slender wrist as the girl extended her arm. A large crescent-shaped mark was visible above her wrist as the sleeve rode up. Suma's eyes were greedy with curiosity.

'You may leave now, child,' Asandhimitra said.

The girl fled the room.

'Is she the one?' the queen asked.

Suma looked disconcerted.

Asandhimitra continued, 'She accompanied us here from Pataliputra. With rumours like these flying about Magadha, Lord Suma, we are glad she did. She is better off here.'

'She resembles someone I know,' Suma said

thoughtfully, regaining his composure. 'Is she from the deep south? From Lanka, perhaps? It's a pity I couldn't see her face. Some years ago, General Nandidevi appointed me to the court of King Devanapriya, the ruler of Lanka. I remember seeing his daughter at play with her pet deer in the garden. Your girl looks very much like her.'

'Perhaps, Lord Suma, perhaps.'

'I also heard a Lankan princess has recently arrived in Pataliputra, bringing a message of peace from her father to King Ashoka. Perhaps it's the same girl I just met.'

'Who told you that a Lankan princess is in Magadha to meet the king?' the Brahmin broke in.

Suma shrugged. 'We have excellent relations with Lanka, both in trade and diplomacy. One hears so many things.'

'We have received no such report,' Asandhimitra said firmly.

'The girl I just saw…'

'She is an orphan, the daughter of one of our noblemen. Both her parents died in a boat accident and I took her under my protection.'

'In which case, I would be honoured to ask for her hand on King Strutayush's behalf, as one of his cherished queens.'

An impish smile appeared on Asandhimitra's lips.

'Why not? We shall make sure she is ready to leave for Kalinga by the time your work here is done,' she said, signalling that the audience was over. She added graciously, 'Rooms have been prepared for you. We are privileged to have such eminent guests.'

The Brahmin added, 'Guards must be posted outside the suites of our honoured visitors, Your Majesty. These are dangerous times as the ambassador says, and we don't want any harm to come to him.'

Suma protested, 'I am sure there is no need for that, Your Majesty. We are staying at the viceroy's…'

'I insist. The Brahmin is right, the palace is a much safer place, especially after your talk of murder in the harem. You must stay here until you accompany Devavarman to Pataliputra,' the queen said calmly, clapping her hands. A court attendant stepped forward. 'Please show them to their chambers and care for them well. They are our guests,' she ordered.

Suma bowed ingratiatingly, and the Brahmin guessed his mind was churning, rapidly weighing his options. Being the queen's guest meant he and Mur would be constantly under the Brahmin's watchful eye. Especially after Mur's botched attempt on his life, Suma must know this was not a good thing. Suma visibly gathered himself and thanked the queen, saying, 'I am grateful for both your solicitude and the gift of the girl. I would also like to inform you that King Srutayush has sent a present for you. It is on its way here. Initially, I wanted to bring it to Pataliputra, but then I was told you would be in Ujjain…'

The Brahmin realized Suma had known all along that the queen would be in Ujjain. Which meant Kalinga's agents had penetrated the palace; perhaps, even the harem. He had to put more security measures in place. But for now, Suma could not be allowed to leave Ujjain and communicate with his spies.

'So, where is your gift? Here, or in Pataliputra?' the Brahmin asked, a tad ungraciously. Asandhimitra shot him a warning look. Suma pretended not to notice.

'It's on its way to Ujjain, Your Majesty and will reach in time for your birthday tomorrow. I beg you to accept it as a token of respect and affection from our king, from one royal to another,' he said.

She inclined her head gracefully.

The Brahmin noticed a flicker in Suma's eyes, malevolent and triumphant. It disappeared as quickly as it had appeared. Asandhimitra swept out of the room, with the Brahmin and Hao following behind. Upon reaching her chamber, she sank into a low divan and buried her face in her hands.

'Suma is an evil man, I can see that. I am worried, Brahmin,' she said. 'I see darkness closing around the kingdom.'

'I will protect it with my life,' the Brahmin said. 'As you do, too. Isn't it wonderful what a pretty veil and a little paint can do?'

Asandhimitra looked up at him frowning. Then she leaned back and began to laugh.

'If only I could see Suma's face when he discovers the identity of the girl he wants as his king's wife,' she said in between un-queenly giggles. 'Very little gets past you, spymaster. Though it was you who ordered Antochlius to bring her to Ujjain, how did you recognize her? You had never met her.'

'Ah, the dancing girl,' the Brahmin said with a laugh.

He wondered how the queen knew he had never

met her. He smiled noncommittally and said, 'Quite a stunt you pulled back there, Your Majesty. But you have to be more careful in future. Suma would have called your bluff if he hadn't been so flustered.'

'Careful? How?'

'She should have worn something on her feet. While everyone was looking at her arm, I was looking at her feet. Her toenails were chipped and her toes were a little splayed. Daughters of aristocrats and the women of the palace don't have imperfect feet.'

'Do you always see what others don't, spymaster?'

'People see only what they are shown, not what they can observe.'

'You are right, but desperate times call for desperate charades. I have to rest now. All this has given me a headache. I'll summon you in the evening.'

The Brahmin did not move. Asandhimitra got up, annoyed.

'Is this how you did it?' he asked, holding up the perfumed veil from the Garden of Secrets.

'Did what?' Asandhimitra raised a delicate eyebrow.

'Summoned me to Ujjain.'

The queen plucked the cloth from the Brahmin's hand.

'Yes, it seemed the best way to lead you to me,' she replied with a mischievous smile. 'Antochlius kept me abreast of developments in the palace after the concubine's murder.'

'So Antochlius was in your pay, Your Majesty?'

Her eyes flashed. 'He is not in my pay, he loves his queen,' she said.

'Forgive me, Your Majesty,' the spymaster murmured softly.

He then apprised her of the young Greek's death. The queen's brow clouded in dismay. She said, 'Dark forces are gathering in Pataliputra. With the king preparing for war, he needs the support of the people. The murder of one of his women can be exploited by our enemies to spread fear and suspicion in the kingdom. Talk travels faster in Magadha than Ashoka's stallions. Once the story gets around that you are investigating the discovery of a veil that could be mine, found near the Chief Eunuch's corpse, people will see Ashoka as an impartial king. I want them to know that even the queen is not above the law. Our enemies will have little to say then. Ashoka can't afford the people distrusting him. Or me.'

The Brahmin felt reluctant admiration for her skill for dissimulation.

'Antochlius was working for me too,' she continued. 'He kept me appraised of the king's plans. So I decided to involve you in plans of my own.'

'Antochlius spied on the king for you?'

'Ashoka discusses weighty matters with his ministers and generals. Being a royal bodyguard, Antochlius was always around,' she replied. 'I made sure he was constantly on the roster. You are not the only one who has friends in low places.'

'The king's secret conclaves are guarded by my men, who are chosen for their loyalty and ability to keep their mouths shut,' the Brahmin said brusquely.

Asandhimitra frowned. 'Antochlius was loyal to you,

spymaster. Blindly. But he had one weakness. He was smitten by one of my serving girls. I told him anything could happen to her in such a large palace building, and who would miss a poor servant? I left him with no choice,' she said.

The Brahmin made a mental note to thoroughly vet the palace guards.

'I hope he was your only spy, my queen,' he said. 'I'm sorry he won't be serving you anymore.'

Asandhimitra nodded sadly.

'What do you have in mind for the princess?' he asked.

'Ah, the princess?' Asandhimitra cocked her eyebrow. 'All in good time, spymaster,' she said wryly, with a smile.

'I need to know, Your Majesty. My investigation depends—'

She cut him short. 'You will know when the time is right.' Her eyes were no longer friendly. The Brahmin considered showing her Ashoka's ring, then decided against it.

'I am sure you will do the right thing when the time comes, as will I,' the queen said. She smiled, illuminating the hall for a brief moment, and left for her private chambers.

'What a remarkable woman,' the Brahmin said aloud. 'No wonder Ashoka loves her so much.'

'With Suma prowling around, we should warn the princess,' Hao interrupted. 'Assuming you know where to find her.'

'All in good time, as the queen said.' The spymaster clapped Hao affectionately on her shoulder. 'The game has just begun.'

Viceroy's Endgame

The night was a dark cowl closing over the land. The Brahmin and Hao were on the stone portico of the east-wing tower of the palace, right below the queen's quarters. The Ujjain palace, where Asandhimitra stayed for most part of the year, was made of stone, though its inner walls were lined with polished teak overlaid with panels of fragrant sandalwood. Ashoka had a fascination for stand-alone pillars. The sprawling grounds of his palaces teemed with them, polished to such perfection that they looked lacquered. The palace gardens, too, were expansive, covering hundreds of square stadia, full of fountains, patios and walkways. And, of course, more pillars.

The Brahmin watched the sleeping city sprawled before him. Here and there, small rectangles of light showed – sleepless residents reading the scriptures, playing chess or making love to their wives or mistresses. Beyond the city, protected by spiked iron railings, lay the moat, its irregular edges pencilled by the moon. In it, pink lotuses bloomed and crocodiles dozed, their bellies full with the flesh of convicts. The Brahmin watched the lazy curve of the Shipra, gleaming like a courtesan's silver girdle. Far away, the forest watched the city, like a great army frozen by a warlock's enchantment, ready to break loose and advance the moment the spell was broken. Lights from the cave dwellings that Queen Devi had built for Buddhist monks punctuated the sloping mass of the hillsides.

Immediately upon reaching Ujjain, the Brahmin had sent a wagon to bring Antochlius's body for cremation. From the portico, he could see the glowing embers of his funeral pyre on the riverbank.

'There will be many more cremations by the time the war is over. Thousands, I suppose,' Hao remarked.

'Hopefully none of them will be ours,' the Brahmin responded.

His thoughts were interrupted by the arrival of a guard, summoning him to the queen's quarters. She was pacing up and down furiously in her chamber.

'He hasn't come,' she said, anger burning in her voice.

'Who?'

'Devavarman. How dare he disobey me?'

'Shall I bring him?'

'I have already dispatched soldiers to his house. They have been ordered to drag him down the streets if he refuses to come.'

'Something is wrong, Your Majesty. He wouldn't dare ignore your summons.'

As if on cue, loud knocks interrupted their conversation. The Brahmin went across and opened the door. An officer stood outside. His face was ashen.

'The viceroy is dead,' he whispered hoarsely.

'How?'

'When we reached his palace, the servants informed us that he was in his suite. We sent the head steward to his room, but he found the door locked. He knocked, but there was no answer. Then we broke down the door and found the viceroy lying dead on the floor, naked. He had fallen from his bed. His skin was blue all over, as if a cobra had attacked him. A wine cup lay near his hand. Wine had spilled on the floor. Another cup stood on a bedside table. It was empty. And the window was open, although it was cold outside.'

'Poisoned?' Asandhimitra asked, taken aback by the news.

The officer shrugged helplessly. 'I don't know, Your Majesty. His quarters are a mess. The mattress on the bed had been shredded with a knife. Cushions had been ripped open, their stuffing strewn all over the floor. Tables lay overturned and scrolls and parchments were scattered everywhere. The treasury chest was open. But no money seems to have been stolen,' he said.

'Really? What has been taken, then?'

The soldier shrugged in dismay. Asandhimitra's rage was as famous as her kindness.

'Did you look for a secret chamber in the box?' the Brahmin broke in.

'No. I didn't know there was one.'

'All treasury chests have false bottoms or hidden panels.'

Asandhimitra turned towards the Brahmin with a wordless command. He left the room, ordering the officer to follow him. They made for the stables, drawing their cloaks tight against the chill. As they galloped through the city, making for its gates and the viceroy's villa ahead, Ujjain was settling down for the night. A few shops were still open, the merchants poring over their books, calculating the profits of the day by the light of oil lamps. Young men in smart clothes drove their chariots along the paved roads, wafting perfume and singing bawdy songs on their way to the pleasure houses of the Courtesan's Quarters. A drunk aristocrat swayed along on a painted howdah atop his elephant. A whore whistled at him and bared her breasts, but at the approach of the horses, she quickly slipped away into a side lane. If caught by the night patrol, she would face a punishment of twenty lashes. Her head would be shaved and she would be cast out of the city to fend for herself. It was the law. A pair of mounted policemen passed the Brahmin and his companion, and whipped their horses around threateningly. Glimpsing the officer's uniform, they turned away with muttered apologies that sounded more like curses.

The two riders thundered over the wooden drawbridge across the moat outside the city walls, towards the suburbs where the wealthier men had their estates. Soon, they glimpsed the viceroy's villa; a big white building protected by tall, thick hedges covered with flowering vines. The officer had left sentries at the entrance to prevent anyone from entering. Or leaving.

The riders clattered into a large stone-paved courtyard encircled by flowerbeds, in the midst of which a fountain sparkled joyously, unmindful of the bloody scene inside the house. The officer led the Brahmin up a wide carpeted staircase and stopped at a high ivory-inlaid door.

'Here we are, the viceroy's suite,' he announced.

The Brahmin entered a large sitting room, taking in the chaos. The remains of a fire lay smouldering in a gigantic fireplace. Silver urns had been toppled from their pedestals. Decanters and cups lay shattered on the floor, their contents staining the big Armenian rugs, which would have cost a servant a year's wages and more. The scene in the bedroom was the same. Paintings in golden frames hung lopsided on the walls, some of them slashed to strips. Furniture was strewn about as if a small storm had just left the room. The air smelt faintly of sex. Devavarman's naked corpse lay on the floor beside the high, canopied mahogany bed, his head lolled back, his face twisted in a grimace of pain. His arm was stretched out, his hand like a claw reaching for the fallen wine cup that lay on its side, almost within the grasp of his splayed fingers. Even in death, it seemed he was desperate for a last drink. The Brahmin picked up the cup and sniffed it. He smiled grimly.

'Poison?' the officer asked.

The Brahmin nodded.

'How did the killer enter the room, you think? Through the window?'

'He *left* through the window but must have come in through a secret door. These palace rooms are full of secrets, and some of them have hidden passageways that lead outside. Let's see.'

The Brahmin walked around the room, pressing his hand down gently on wall panels and probing the joints with his feet. Then he inspected the fireplace carefully. He peered at each stone, and one in particular seemed to interest him. Gingerly, he pressed on it. The whole fireplace slid aside noiselessly, exposing a doorway behind. The surprised officer gave a low whistle and peered in.

'But why did the killer not get out of the room through this?' he asked.

'The killer did.'

'Then why was the window left open?'

'Mere distraction, meant to confuse us. If you follow the passageway, you will see it leads outside the walls of the palace.' And it did.

In a corner of the viceroy's room stood a big, broad royal treasury chest. Its lid was open. Precious stones, coins of gold, silver and copper, and piles of ornaments spilled out of it.

'This box was opened with a key,' the Brahmin declared.

'How is that possible, sir? Where could the robbers have got a key?'

'Notice the knife marks on the lid? These too are meant to fool us. Now, check the keyhole; not a single scratch anywhere around it. Not even a little mark. This mess is another diversion.'

Diversion and deception, the timeless weapons of espionage.

'None of the gems and coins lying around have been taken. So what's gone?' the officer asked.

Without saying a word, the Brahmin heaved the box on to its side. The remaining treasure emptied on the floor. He crouched on his heels beside the box and using the tip of his dagger, applied gentle pressure on the wooden studs that held the bottom down. Suddenly, with a loud click, a false bottom flipped down, revealing a small chamber beneath.

From it, a kovidara dropped on the floor.

'Wait outside in the hall,' he ordered the officer.

He kept the flower aside and placed the box back upright. He probed it further. His search was rewarded with a piece of paper, caught in a crack between the false bottom and the main chamber. His eyes narrowed as he studied it.

'Back to the palace, there is no time to lose!' he snapped, striding out of the room. A young servant girl appeared from behind a pillar. His hand went to his sword.

'Hush, master, it's me.' She held a finger to her lips. He recognized her as one of his spies in the viceroy's house. She whispered in his ear. He nodded and reached for his pocket. 'Well done,' he whispered, but she had already taken the money and vanished.

Downstairs, the servants had been herded into a corner of the foyer by the guards. He questioned each of them in detail, though he was sure nothing would come of it. The Brahmin had met other killers like the Blood Flower, although none as mysterious and accomplished. They did not work with accomplices. They were too arrogant, and too sure of their lethal skills to seek help. Naturally, nobody in Devavarman's house had seen or heard anything.

Upon returning to the city, the Brahmin was met by one of his spies at the palace gate. His face grew grim, as he listened to the story of another murder. One of his men. Suma has much to answer for, he thought darkly. When he arrived at the queen's quarters at last, she was up, waiting for him.

'It's true. Devavarman is dead. He was poisoned.' He held out the kovidara from the treasure chest.

Asandhimitra gave a small cry of surprise. 'Was it the Blood Flower?' she asked.

'Perhaps. The killer used a key to open the treasure chest.'

'How? Was Devavarman tortured for the key?'

'There were no signs of torture. He never took the key home. It was always kept in his office, which is guarded round the clock by armed soldiers. The king's taxes and tithes are stored inside. No money seems to have been taken from the chest either.'

Asandhimitra shivered and crossed her arms.

"But I know what has been taken from the box,' the Brahmin said confidently. 'Sometimes even the best of killers are too clever by half.' He showed her the piece of paper he had retrieved from the treasure chest.

'What is this?'

'Ashoka's war plans for the invasion of Kalinga, if I am correct. Didn't Devavarman tell us he had gone to Pataliputra to meet the king? It was no ordinary meeting. It was a war council. My spies had told me that a copy of the plans was given to each Aryaputra to coordinate the movement of troops, money and supply routes when the invasion happens.'

'Who do you think stole the plans and killed Devavarman?'

'The Kalingans are my best bet. Do you see a woman

like Mur falling in love with a lout like Devavarman, if you will excuse my description? It looks like the Blood Flower is here after all, working for the Kalingans. And my guess is that it's Suma who hired the assassin, not Nandidevi. No doubt the stolen papers are hidden somewhere in Suma's room.'

'If that's the case wouldn't Suma have asked the Blood Flower to take the air plans to Nandidevi immediately?'

The Brahmin shook his head. 'Suma is too arrogant to let it happen. He would want to give the war plans to Nandidevi himself and take the credit. The man is as vain as a peacock.

'But how can we search his rooms? It would be a breach of protocol, especially at such a sensitive time. Then again, if we don't find the plans, Magadha is in trouble. I must go to Pataliputra to warn the king,' Asandhimitra said, rising from her seat.

'There is another way, Your Majesty,' the Brahmin said.

'Which is?'

'We make our own version of the war plans and plant them on Suma.'

'But how?'

'If they are in his room, or on his person, Hao will find them. You just need to keep the two Kalingans occupied for a few hours.'

Asandhimitra's posture relaxed. She tilted her head back and gave an unladylike roar of laughter.

'No wonder Ashoka loves you. Your cunning would flummox the wiliest fox.'

'Ashoka prefers to call me his wolf,' the Brahmin said a bit reproachfully. The queen smiled.

'All right, my royal wolf, what do you want from me?'

'Some parchment, just like the one here,' he said, showing her the torn paper. 'It's used in the royal household. I have carried the king's messages many times, I know.'

'But will Suma not be able to tell the difference between the two plans?'

'I doubt it. Most of the royal scribes have similar writing, thanks to the king's passion for order. Suma is no fool, but he also thinks there is no man or woman in the world who can outsmart him. Besides, he is sure nobody will dare enter his room as long as he is your guest. If I hadn't discovered the piece of paper in the treasury box, I would never have guessed the plans had been stolen. Now we know. But Suma doesn't know we know.'

Asandhimitra went across to a desk and took out a sheaf of parchments, an inkpot and some quills.

'These are yours, spymaster. Meanwhile, I will send a messenger to inform Mur that her lover is dead and there will be no marriage between Kalinga and Magadha,' she said.

'I request you to wait till the morning,' the Brahmin said. 'We must first send a message to Pataliputra with the news. The king should be warned.'

The queen agreed and the Brahmin took her leave.

Upon reaching his room, he rubbed smooth the parchments Asandhimitra had given him with a pumice stone, spreading them out carefully on a desk. He dipped a quill in the inkpot and began work, a mischievous smile playing on his lips. Outside in the retreating night, an owl hooted, like an envoy of death.

The War Plans Vanish

It was in a sombre mood that Queen Asandhimitra, the Brahmin and Hao, along with the two Kalingans, assembled in the morning room. Devavarman's death had affected them all in different ways. Suma's weary face suggested a sleepless night, but each time he glanced at the spymaster, his eyes glittered with barely concealed triumph.

'If he only knew what we've been up to, he wouldn't be feeling so good,' the Brahmin thought to himself.

Suma had been busy after his audience with the queen the previous morning. The spy who met the Brahmin at the city gate on his return from Devavarman's villa had informed him that a cloaked figure had left Suma's quarters soon afterwards, and vanished into the crowded streets. Someone had reported seeing a similar figure on a horse, racing away in the direction of the viceroy's villa. His men had spent the day searching the city, but could not gather any relevant information. The spy also told him that Suma had later received a nocturnal visitor, a junior Kalingan diplomat who left after a hurried conference.

Now, as he regarded the Kalingan envoy in the breakfast room, the Brahmin's face was impassive. Beside him sat Hao, the ivory hilt of her dagger protruding from her belt. Weapons were not allowed in the presence of the king or the queen, but the Brahmin and his assistant were exceptions. Mur was absent from the table.

Suma cleared his throat.

'I'm sorry to hear about what happened last night,' he said.

'What happened?' the Brahmin inquired softly.

'I heard the viceroy is dead. My niece is distraught, she cried all night. I had to give her a sleeping draught. I apologize for her absence.'

'We are sorry to hear that,' the queen responded. 'She must rest.'

Suma shook his head regretfully.

'I am afraid I have to send her to Pataliputra today, this terrible tragedy has shaken her. But I will be staying back for your birthday celebrations, Your Majesty.'

'I cannot allow Mur to leave until I am satisfied she is well enough to travel. I shall send my own physician to examine her,' the queen replied.

Suma looked alarmed. Asandhimitra then summoned her physician – a tall, stooping man with a kind face and piercing eyes. She whispered in his ear. He bowed and left the room, accompanied by two soldiers and a palace maid.

'I am sure this isn't necessary,' Suma protested. 'Mur is young. She must be better already.'

'I thought she was devastated,' Hao pointed out.

Suma started to say something more but Asandhimitra raised her hand, ending the conversation. She ordered breakfast to be served. Servants poured in, bearing trays of fragrant dishes – duck roasted in honey, braised fish sprinkled with gold dust on a bed of rose petals, spicy chicken morsels on a gold salver in the shape of

Magadha, quail in saffron sauce garnished with onion and red chillies from the north-east, and thin slices of mutton cooked in milk seasoned with cinnamon. Two swans of spun sugar arrived on a bed of ice, embedded with one large diamond each to resemble an eye. Their beaks were painted red with pomegranate paste. Fragrant long-grained rice cooked with spiced minced meat and sprinkled with mint leaves was placed in an oblong silver dish in the centre of the table. Oranges from faraway Gaul, bananas and pears from the south of Bharatvarsh, grapes from Greece and sweet lemon from China filled golden bowls encrusted with jade, sapphire and amethyst. Two servants waited upon each guest, one holding an amphora of wine while the other carried a huge jar of mint tea.

'Even in the midst of tragedy we must nourish our bodies,' Asandhimitra declared to Suma. 'Without a strong body, there cannot be a strong mind. Let's eat.'

Suma looked mournfully at the food and nodded. The servants began to fill the plates, and the company settled down. Soon, the pallor had left Suma's face and the pink returned to his cheeks.

'Your Majesty is most kind, thinking of our welfare when the viceroy has been murdered so brutally,' he said.

'Who said he was murdered?' interrupted the Brahmin sharply.

Suma looked taken aback, then said, 'The queen sent us the news of his death. My niece heard it and fainted.'

'You haven't answered me, my lord,' the Brahmin persisted.

'I simply guessed...'

'Last night, the queen sent a messenger to Pataliputra with the news that Aryaputra Devavarman was dead,' the Brahmin said in a low voice underlaid with steel. 'Not that he was murdered.'

The spy at the gate had told the Brahmin that the messenger had been waylaid by Kalingan spies, interrogated and killed. Suma had been briefed by the junior diplomat he had met in secret afterwards, who suffered a similar fate at the hands of the Brahmin's men. Such was the fate of spies.

The Kalingan ambassador nervously licked away a stray crystal of sugar at the corner of his mouth. Then he recovered his poise. He said, 'Devavarman was young and healthy. Why, we met him only yesterday. He seemed in high spirits. He presented Mur with a golden ring set with a huge red ruby. Why would such a healthy man die so unexpectedly unless something suspicious happened to him?'

'Maybe something suspicious did happen,' Hao said drily, rising from her seat. Suma looked alarmed.

'Where are you off to?' he asked sharply. Hao gave him an innocent, dimpled smile.

'Isn't it rude, my lord, to ask young girls where they are going? There are certain days in the month when you should not be asking such questions.' Suma blushed. Hao ignored him and bowed to the queen. 'If Your Majesty permits, I would like to rest a bit,' she said in a girlish voice. 'I am not feeling too well. A little dizzy…'

The queen smiled and summoned her maids, who quickly rushed to the Viet girl's side.

'Take her to the infirmary and give her a herb infusion,' the queen ordered. Suma followed Hao's departure with anxious eyes.

'A sharp man,' the Brahmin thought. 'He thinks she's faking it. He's worried she'll steal into Mur's chamber and find the war plans.'

Mur, of course, would be fast asleep, having been sedated by the queen's physician.

Noting Suma's obvious discomfort, Asandhimitra cleared her throat.

'Hao will be fine. Let us return to our earlier conversation, Lord Suma. How did you know Devavarman was murdered?'

'I could not sleep, Your Majesty,' Suma answered. 'I was standing by the window, looking out. The night was so peaceful. Then I heard the rush of horses in the palace courtyard, and the excited voices of soldiers. I heard the Viceroy's name being mentioned. Soon afterwards, I saw the Brahmin, accompanied by an officer, leave in a hurry. I wondered what the commotion was about. In the morning, when the news of the viceroy's death was conveyed to me, I simply put two and two together. I am a seasoned diplomat and have lived long and seen much. It wasn't a difficult conclusion to arrive at.'

Suma wiped his lips and leaned back against the cushions with a satisfied sigh.

The man is a superb liar, the Brahmin thought with reluctant admiration. A less experienced or intelligent person would have found himself in an uncomfortable position. But he had evaded the trap swiftly and smartly.

'You are perceptive,' the Brahmin commented quietly.

'We diplomats are trained to observe small things in the big picture. Understanding the present and anticipating the future is what diplomacy is all about.'

Asandhimitra applauded softly. 'Your perspicacity is admirable, Lord Suma. Come, let us finish our breakfast and then take a walk in the garden. I have many questions for you.'

Suma looked around him, searching for a way to escape. Looking for a way to get to his rooms and check on the war plans, the Brahmin guessed. He felt proud that Asandhimitra was playing the game well.

'May I see if Mur is all right first?' asked Lord Suma.

The queen shook her head prettily. 'You do not have to worry about her, she is in capable hands. My physician is the best in all of Magadha. Also, sentries have been posted outside her room to ensure nobody gets in,' she said.

'Or out,' the Brahmin added with a smile.

Asandhimitra invited the two men to follow her. 'Come, the palace garden is delightful at this time of the year,' she said. 'The flowering plants have been imported from all over the world. It is a place for reflection. There is even a maze, which the king designed himself because he is very good with puzzles. Do you like mazes, Lord Suma?'

'Not really,' the diplomat smiled. 'Mazes are for lovers and spies. I am neither, just a humble diplomat who would get lost in a maze, however small it may be.'

He was looking more relaxed. The Brahmin knew

why. Suma did not have to worry about the Brahmin breaking into his rooms as long as they were both with the queen.

Asandhimitra would have made a good spy had she not been a queen, the Brahmin thought, shaking his head in admiration as he followed her onto the wide marble terrace that led out into the garden.

Gravelled paths ran at right angles between bright flowerbeds of all hues. Dragonflies hovered over lotus ponds. The air was redolent with the heady fragrance of jasmine stirred with roses. Dappled sunlight sprinkled the pathways. The queen led them to a frangipani grove with two marble benches facing each other. She invited Suma to sit opposite her. The Brahmin stood beside her, staring at an invisible spot above the envoy's head. Resting an elbow on her knee, the queen placed her chin on her small fist and gazed at Suma speculatively.

'Tell me, ambassador, will there be war?' she asked.

Suma started.

'Of course not, Your Majesty. We are neighbors who live side by side in harmony, in spite of a previous misunderstanding with King Chandragupta. But the great Ashoka is a man of peace.'

The queen smiled.

'A misunderstanding! That's a good one, Suma. Only a diplomat would call an invasion a misunderstanding.'

Suma gave a narrow smile.

'Is it not an exaggeration, calling the king a man of peace?' Asandhimitra continued. 'The brutal conquest of Taxila, the merciless suppression of the Ujjain revolt, the massacre of his brother's army and his subsequent murder are not signs of a man of peace. Tens of thousands of people have died in my lord's wars.'

'We speak of the past, Your Majesty. Men change, even kings,' the ambassador replied in a honeyed tone. 'Did the king's grandfather not become a Jain monk, a man of peace? I have heard of a Holy One from the land of the Buddha, who now travels across Magadha, preaching non-violence. Perhaps he will meet the king one day.'

'Do not ever speak of the Sakyamuni in my presence,' the queen lashed out in sudden fury.

The Brahmin gave Suma a warning look. He knew Asandhimitra felt slighted by Ashoka's first wife, Devi, who was a follower of the Buddha. When Ashoka became king, he had wanted to take Prince Mahendra to Pataliputra to be groomed as his heir, but Devi was aware that the king's lust for war would not be satiated until he, like Alexander, had conquered the world. She had refused. Asandhimitra had promised to bring up Mahendra like her own son, but she did not relent.

'The great Ashoka will never harm our country,' Suma declared. 'Isn't Princess Kaurwaki of Kalinga his third queen?'

Asandhimitra shrugged as if the number of queens Ashoka had was not her concern.

The Brahmin heard the rustle of leaves behind him. Hao stepped into the grove and curtsied to the queen. Suma looked annoyed.

'I see you are fine now,' he said spitefully.

'I am, my lord, thank you,' Hao said demurely.

'Thanks to the herbal potions the physicians gave me, I've never felt better.'

Suma turned his head away. Hao winked at the Brahmin. The queen noticed, smiled and stood up from her seat.

'We are honoured that your king has sent us a gift, and look forward to seeing it,' she told Suma. 'We also invite you to share our private enclosure at my birthday celebrations. After that, you and your niece can leave for Kalinga, provided she is well enough to travel.'

'Why, thank you, Your Majesty. I am sure Mur will be better, especially since Your Majesty has such fine physicians,' Suma replied. 'Also, a messenger has informed me that the gift intended for your birthday has reached the Ujjain port already. It has been made by Kalinga's best craftsmen and I hope you will like it. I am sleepless with excitement,' he purred.

'We look forward to seeing it,' Asandhimitra said and held out her hand. The diplomat went down on his knees to kiss it. The queen inclined her head gracefully and walked away. The Brahmin turned to Suma.

'What is this precious gift you speak of?' he said sarcastically. 'Even I'm so excited I won't be able to sleep.'

'You'll have to wait. Now I have to go and see how my niece is doing.'

'I wonder what the old fox is up to,' the Brahmin said aloud as Hao and he watched Lord Suma's retreating back.

'Whatever it is, can't be good,' Hao said. 'But all news is not bad news.'

She took out a roll of parchment from the pocket of her pantaloons.

'I knew you would find it,' the Brahmin said triumphantly. 'Where was it hidden?'

'In a cavity inside the hilt of Suma's ceremonial sword. The sword was in its scabbard, which was tied to the iron brackets on the wall with a leather string in a tight Kalinga knot.'

'What do you know about Kalinga knots?'

'It's a numbered knot, and the combination is known only to the one who has tied it. Find the hidden loops in the knots first, pull the string out through them and the knot unravels. Easy. I've seen such knots before. In another time, another place.'

The Brahmin refrained from asking her any more. The woman was full of surprises.

'And you just happened to decode it,' he said ironically.

She shrugged modestly.

'Yes, but it took some hard thinking. I tried all sorts of combinations, from the letters in Kalinga, its king's name, Suma's own name and even the number of spies in the Kalinga Secret Service, which you had told me the other day. Once I recalled that the documents were stolen from Devavarman's palace, I looked for the numbers of letters in Devavarman's name. That didn't work either. Then I remembered they were to marry on the tenth day of the tenth month. I divided ten by two, for Mur and him, which thankfully proved to be the right combination. I found the five loops after some probing, and I pulled the business end of the string through them. And ho! The sword was free! Exchanging the documents and retying the knot was child's play.'

'Clever. I'm glad you didn't follow Alexander's example of the Gordian knot.'

'Cutting the knots certainly would've been easier, but it would've defeated the purpose, don't you think? Now, shall I take these away to my room and burn them?' she asked teasingly, reaching for the plans. The Brahmin shook his head.

'No. It's always good to have some leverage over the king. We don't know when we'll need it.'

'You don't trust anyone, do you?' Hao asked.

'Especially not the king. But some I do, my she-wolf.'

For the first time, he saw Hao blush. The Brahmin pretended not to have noticed. He said, 'One of my spies at the viceroy's house said the forest between the palace and the port is full of Kalingan soldiers, led by a tall Greek captain. From her description I guessed it must be Telemachus. Hidden among the trees, she also saw a massive object covered with heavy hemp cloth, which was being guarded by the soldiers night and day. But she couldn't get any closer.'

Hao nodded briskly, the blush having disappeared from her cheeks.

'The gift?' she said in a thoughtful voice.

'Could be. But where Lord Suma is involved, nothing is what it is. It's time we discovered more about this mysterious gift. Remember, some gifts bring happiness and some bring grief.'

'Then I better go and see what grief Suma is planning for Magadha.'

'Don't get caught.'

Hao threw a pitying look at her master, as if he had said something extremely foolish. He laughed.

'Careful, the forest is full of Kalingan soldiers. And Telemachus,' he said.

'Then let's hope Telemachus's sake that he doesn't meet me,' she said, fingering the hilt of her dagger, and left for the stables, looking for her horse.

From some distant garden, a sharika bird gave a sharp warning cry, having spotted a serpent writhing its way towards an unsuspecting field mouse.

Royal Apprehensions

As if Devavarman's ghost lingered in the dusk outside, dinner was a subdued affair. It was served in the queen's dining chamber, which was not as grand as the main dining hall. Its arched windows were shielded with bamboo panels covered by fragrant sheets of khus grass, held in place by strips of red silk. As the breeze slipped in through the slits, shivering with Shipra's kisses, the spicy sweet scent of khus wafted through the chamber. Servants dressed in the queen's blue-and-silver livery waited on them, serving fragrant rice spiced with cardamom and lemon pickle. The meal was sparse and vegetarian, with side dishes of lentil with roasted asafoetida and cottage cheese dipped in tomato gravy.

Mur was again absent. Suma apologised profusely for her absence, explaining that she was still indisposed, and that her grief over Devavarman's death had disturbed her body's humours. But the ambassador's tone was jaunty. His eyes crinkled merrily.

'You look happy, Lord Suma,' Asandhimitra observed.

'I am looking forward to your birthday celebrations.'

'As I am looking forward to your mysterious present.'

'Half the joy is in the waiting, Your Majesty,' Suma said.

The Brahmin smiled to himself. The man looks smug, he thought. Which meant the strategy of switching the war plans had worked. He does not suspect a thing. The Brahmin was certain the Kalingan had hurried to his room after his conversation with the queen in the garden the previous day and checked the stolen plans. He considered with some amusement the manner in which Hao had turned the tables on one of Kalinga's cleverest minds. He must remember to ask Ashoka to reward her well.

They finished the rest of the meal in silence. As they thanked the queen and departed, Suma threw a triumphant glance at the Brahmin before disappearing through the archway to his room.

'The poor fool,' the Brahmin thought. 'He thinks he has the war plans. How I would like to see his face when the invasion begins.'

The Brahmin bid the queen farewell and made for his favourite watching spot in the palace – a pillared nook in the parapet wall below a watchtower, high above the city. He strolled along the balustered gallery floor, which was lit by torches, his mind churning with thoughts of conspiracies, war and the nature of Suma's mysterious gift. In the courtyards below, interconnected through a series of arched corridors, fountains sent up silver showers from their wide stone basins, palace maids and turbaned attendants went about their chores, guards changed shifts, officials on their way home after conducting the business of the day gossiped about their mundane dealings – the sounds and sights of a great palace slowly preparing for the night. Soon he left the gallery and slipped into a side corridor with a flight of steps that led to a small door. Opening it by pressing a lever on its side, the spymaster entered the walled parapet that ran along the palace roof, interrupted by tall towers from where a lookout could see the city, the silver length of the Shipra and the forest beyond. He took his place in a sheltered nave, leaned back against the wall and watched the night fall over the city.

Like all the great cities in the kingdom, Ujjain, too, was protected by bamboo-spiked ditches, moats and ramparts. Three concentric walls of earth, wood and brick surrounded it. Drainage from homes and palaces led into the outer moat. The homes of the aristocrats, imitating the architectural style of the royal palace, had battlements, towers, covered walkways and watergates. Somewhere a portcullis groaned as it rose grudgingly. Horses clattered on the wide street along the inner city wall. It was the night watch; soldiers from gulmas in different quarters of the city.

Houses big and small, made of wood and brick, wore a sense of quietude, although occasionally the illuminated window of a two- or three-storey building rectangulated the night. It was forbidden by law for the front windows of opposite houses to overlook each other. They also had to face the streets. The head of the household was required to sleep in the forequarters of his home, ready to be woken at a moment's notice if an alarm was raised over a fire or a robbery. Thousands of water pots filled to the brim lined the streets, for the wooden houses were apt to catch fire quickly. The punishment for arson was death: the culprit would be burned alive.

Like any Magadhan city, Ujjain, too, was organized

into palaces, workshops, granaries, armouries and gaols. Tonight, a group of unfortunates was being walked single-file to prison – a sorry procession of prostitutes, pimps, outlaws and thieves. The pimps would be strapped to wooden frames and their bodies smeared with excreta. The outlaws and thieves would be hanged from the gallows outside the city walls, their bodies left to rot, to remind everyone of the retribution that awaited those who broke the laws of Magadha.

The gardens of the grand houses of noblemen and rich merchants – with their several courts, built one behind the other – perfumed the air. A trumpet sounded the four-hour nocturnal curfew, after which it was forbidden for a citizen to venture outside.

He thought of Hao's mission in the forest. He had sent her on a dangerous enterprise; if she was captured, Telemachus would show her no mercy.

The spymaster felt a sense of foreboding. Something waited in the forest; something massive and monstrous, fashioned by Lord Suma's twisted mind. He would know soon. As soon as Hao was back.

He felt a hand on his shoulder and turned around, surprised. He had been lost in his thoughts – a mistake no spy should make.

It was Asandhimitra. Her hair was loose and her sheer muslin robe did little to hide the lushness of her figure. The wind rose from the mountains and raced across the Shipra, tossing about droplets like a wet animal, to embrace them. Asandhimitra shivered and crossed her arms over her breasts.

'I am afraid, spymaster,' she said. 'I am afraid for the king, for myself and Magadha.'

'So am I. But fear is of no use. To be afraid of danger is to be wise, but to yield to fear is fatal.'

'You are a loyal friend,' she said, placing her hand on his shoulder again and smiling at him. He wanted to gather and fold the slender frame into his arms, and kiss the full lips that would taste of honey and wine. But he kept his face impassive and his body still, not allowing his emotions to show. 'What is it about this woman that makes me feel so protective of her?' he wondered. 'It makes me vulnerable too.'

'In this palace, surrounded by conspiracies, with war in the air and spies everywhere, I feel so alone.' Asandhimitra's soft hand travelled down to the Brahmin's muscular chest. 'I couldn't sleep. Suma makes me uneasy. I fear he is up to something nasty.'

'Do you fear he will harm the princess?' the spymaster asked, stepping away. The queen removed her hand from his chest and shook her head in unspoken warning.

The Brahmin knew it was useless to argue. She was a queen and a very stubborn one. But he continued, 'I have proof that Lord Suma had a hand in Antochlius's death. And the beautiful Mur tried to have me killed. The princess is the key to the mystery. I hope she is safe.'

'She is. There are dark forces at work, spymaster. We are all pieces in Ashoka's game. I often wonder about his purpose. More power? More land? More wealth? More subjects? More deaths? It appears to be a hunger that can never be satisfied.'

'Such is the way of kings, as you know well, Your Majesty. Power is an abyss that can never be filled. War is the destiny of kings. And the peace that follows makes the winners wise and the losers wiser.'

'The wisdom of kings comes at a great cost, spymaster. It comes from the blood of the slain and the cries of widows and orphans. Once they have established their dominance through war, they wish to be worshipped as just rulers.'

She gave a bitter laugh. The Brahmin bowed his head.

'With the war looming over us all, I now understand why Devi would not follow Ashoka, or let him take her children,' Asandhimitra said.

The spy saw the wistful look in his queen's eyes, like a tendril of smoke from a distant forest fire.

'Whatever lies ahead, my lady, I will not let anything happen to you, or to the king,' he said, dropping to one knee. 'I will willingly lay down my life for you.'

Asandhimitra's eyes were wet. She gently touched him on his shoulder again, bidding him to rise. 'I know that,' she said, 'but I don't want you to die for me. I want you to live and serve Magadha for me. For me and the king.'

He thought of Hao's mission and the terrible danger she faced.

For her, too, he whispered to himself.

A Warning in the Night

Far away in Pataliputra, the king tossed restlessly on his bed. The fire in the great hearth of the room was dead, but the glowing orange of the coals kept it warm. The concubine who slept next to him stirred in her sleep. Her leg was out of the goose feather quilt, resting on his heavy thigh. Her silver anklet shone dull in the gloom, like the ghost of an afterthought. He absently caressed her long thick hair fanned out on the pillows. She murmured and flung her hand over his muscular chest. He moved it away, feeling irritated and restless.

'I wonder where that bloody spy of mine is right now,' he said to himself. 'It's time for war. But before that, he had better capture the Blood Flower.'

The bloody spy was standing with the queen on the ramparts of the Ujjain palace, listening to her, nodding occasionally. The queen looked relieved when she finished.

'Now that I have told you everything, remember, she must make it home safe,' Asandhimitra repeated.

'Upon my life, she will, Your Majesty.'

A raven croaked, and Asandhimitra started.

'Ravens remind me of death, spymaster,' she murmured. 'I wonder what tomorrow will bring.'

'Whatever it brings, we will be ready for it, Your Majesty,' he replied.

With a kindness uncharacteristic of a queen,

Asandhimitra touched his cheek lightly and walked away, leaving only the echoes of her silver anklets behind.

The Brahmin returned to his contemplation of the forest. Far above him, the cosmos danced in a swirl of stars and galaxies, dense with the mysteries of planets that decide the fate of mortals. Dawn was breaking over the fields. Emerging from its shimmering distance, a form in black was moving with swift and silent purpose towards the palace of Ujjain like a message from fate.

Suddenly he heard a familiar whirring sound and flung himself down on the floor as a crossbow bolt embedded itself in the wall. He was trapped. If he were to crawl along the corridor to the safety of the doorway, he would not be able to help exposing himself between the stone teeth of the ramparts. He willed his breathing to slow down, till he could hardly feel it. His brain acquired sharper focus and his pulse slowed. He heard the long sharp whistle of the night patrol returning to their gulmas and hoped it would scare the assassin away. But anyone who could use a crossbow bolt with such accuracy had extraordinary eyesight and skill. Only an experienced Greek soldier, or one trained by the Greeks, could have executed a shot like this – considering the only cover from where the missile could have come was beyond the perimeter wall. Telemachus?

The Brahmin flipped over on to his back. In the light of the golden dawn, he noticed a small scroll tied around the bolt stem. He rose cautiously, tensing for the hiss of an approaching bolt. It didn't come. The mysterious archer had vanished. The spymaster withdrew the bolt from the wall, grunting at the effort, and unwrapped the scroll.

Two words were scrawled across it. 'Remember Hecuba.'

'Hecuba? Sounds like Greek. What the hell does it mean?' he wondered.

'I know what it means,' Hao whispered close to his ear, having appeared beside him with characteristic stealth. 'Keeping the company of spies like Antochlius has taught me a thing or two about Greece.'

'How long have you been here?' he asked, annoyed. 'I didn't hear you.'

'That's my secret,' she teased him, pleased.

'Did you discover Suma's secret? His mysterious gift?'

She nodded. His face darkened as he listened.

'If you're right, arrangements have to be made immediately. We need help fast, and I can think of only one person for that,' he said. 'There is no time to be lost. Hao, you have to travel again and this time even further.'

'I'm ready,' she answered.

He gave her quick instructions. Soon he heard the sound of hooves galloping away through the city gates along the long winding road that led away from Ujjain. He watched Hao's receding form, her black cloak billowing behind her like a dark wing, He uttered a prayer, surprising himself.

Maybe this time, he would need the gods on his side. An army would be even better. If Hao was right, the biggest challenge of his career lay ahead.

The sun rose suddenly – a great orange eye – as the earth dipped on its axis. The clouds began to bleed.

The Girl Dies

A day later, Queen Asandhimitra's birthday morning arrived, stained with blood. She had been dreaming of Ashoka on a battlefield, dressed in the saffron robes of a Buddhist monk, head shaven, gripping a great shining sword dripping with blood. Corpses lay scattered around him. She heard the wailing of women beating their chests as crows pecked on the eyes of the dead. In the dream, Ashoka held out a red flower and whispered to her, 'Here, take it, my love, and wear in in your hair. It's a blood flower.'

She woke up with screams ringing in her ears. She reached for the bell rope behind her bed. The door opened and a middle-aged woman came in.

'What is the noise about, Iantha?' Asandhimitra demanded to know.

The woman bowed. 'Another murder,' she said. 'A girl has been killed in the harem.'

Asandhimitra's hand flew to her mouth. Iantha's face looked grim.

She was Asandhimitra's childhood nurse – a Greek woman from Rhodes, whom Mediterranean slave traders had sold to the king of Assandh. Asandhimitra was a quiet child, preferring her own company to that of the children of concubines and dancing girls, or even her own numerous cousins. One day, while playing hopscotch alone in the garden, she accidentally trod on a snake. As it reared up to strike, someone grabbed her from behind. The snake was flung aside but not before it had sunk its fangs into a slim fair arm, which belonged to Iantha.

The poison was strong and Iantha hovered between life and death for many days. The palace physicians bled her, applied poultices to her wound and gave her herbal potions to sleep. Through her poisoned days and nights, she felt the presence of a little girl and the pressure of her small, soft hand on hers. When the fever broke and the poison had dissipated, Iantha realised Asandhimitra had been at her bedside all along. The child had become so attached to her that the king released her from slavery and appointed her as the princess's nurse. When Asandhimitra arrived in Magadha to wed Ashoka, Iantha came with her. She was the only person who called her by her name, except of course the king.

'Hush, Asa,' she crooned now to her agitated mistress, gathering her to her ample bosom as if she were still a child. 'It's your birthday today, my little queen. Nothing should spoil it.'

Asandhimitra shook off Iantha's embrace.

'I am the queen of Magadha and this is my palace, Iantha,' she said in an imperious tone the nurse knew well. 'Tell me, who was killed?'

Even as Iantha started to answer, Asandhimitra interrupted.

'Was it her?' she asked.

'No, Asa, she is safe.' Iantha replied. 'But whenever you plan to send her home, it won't be a day too soon.'

'Then who has been killed?'

'It was the dancing girl Antochlius had brought here from Pataliputra. Two palace ladies on their way to the bathing pool came across her body lying on the patio. Her throat was slit. The harem keeper had to give them opium to shut them up.'

Asandhimitra frowned.

'The poor girl!' she sighed.

'Don't worry. Asa. The Brahmin and his men are already on the scene.'

'Ask him to come here once he is finished,' she ordered. 'He has to get to the bottom of this.'

The nurse left the room and returned with the news that the Brahmin would be with them soon. Tears welled up in the queen's eyes. Iantha held out her arms. She collapsed into them.

'I am frightened, Iantha. A girl has been killed in my own palace, which is guarded by hundreds of soldiers! Do I have to fear for my own life now?'

'Hush, hush, dearest Asa,' the Greek woman whispered gently into her ear. 'It will never come to that.'

Asandhimitra flung herself on the bed, sobbing and clutching her nurse's hands.

'The spymaster will be here soon,' Iantha whispered. 'You must gather yourself, my child. Nobody can be allowed to see a queen like this. Especially Queen Asandhimitra.'

Asandhimitra wiped her cheeks and blew her nose in a most un-queenlike manner. Then she smiled and hugged her nurse.

'You are right. I am going for my bath and you can

dress me afterwards,' she said. 'Ask the Brahmin to wait in my private chamber when he comes.'

When she returned, gone was the distraught woman with fearful eyes and unbound hair. Her head was held high. The fine arches of her eyebrows were drawn with the paste of burnt almonds and ochre. The Brahmin rose respectfully.

'Someone has violated the sanctity of our birthday, Brahmin,' she said, taking a seat on a high-backed chair. 'First a murder in Pataliputra and now in this palace? Why couldn't you stop it?'

The spymaster bowed his head.

'I beg your forgiveness, Your Majesty,' he answered in a low voice. 'I did not anticipate this. I am sure the killer lives in the palace. I promise to find him,' he said.

'How do you know he lives here?'

'Only a trusted member of the royal household can move around the palace freely without attracting attention. This makes him even more dangerous.'

'Do you suspect the Kalingans?'

'They do not need such a distraction. I suspect they have bigger plans. But all is not lost, Your Majesty. May I advise you to give the girl a funeral befitting a Lankan princess? It will confuse Suma.'

Asandhimitra looked shocked for an instant. Then she nodded her assent.

'Was she killed because she resembled someone else?' she demanded.

'No. It was a warning.'

'Meant for?'

'All of us. Do not take what is yours if you do not let me make it mine,' he quoted.

The queen cocked her eyebrow. The Brahmin took out a parchment from his pocket and read aloud: '"Do not take what is yours if you doth not let me make it mine." I found this beside the dancing girl's body. Remember, she was promised to Srutayush? Her murder is a warning to Suma, that he will not get what he wants. And for me to let things be. The killer is threatening to stop anyone from taking what they don't deserve.'

'You mean, the…'

'Perhaps, we cannot rule anything out,' the Brahmin said.

'But how does the killer know? All this is so confusing. Catch the him, and catch him now,' Asandhamitra ordered.

'I will,' he promised. 'I always do.'

'Summon Suma, before he gets to know of the murder from the servants,' the queen said. 'Servants love to gossip, Kalingan or Magadhan.'

The Brahmin agreed. A guard was promptly dispatched to bring Suma. He arrived, accompanied by Mur. All traces of sorrow at Devavarman's murder had vanished from her face. She was impeccably groomed, her cheeks pink with a diluted solution of crushed mulberries, lips painted with red ochre paste. Her slanting eyebrows were penciled together on her forehead with a blend of charcoal and olive oil, in the Greek fashion. A light patina of powdered white lead mixed with water made her skin look even fairer.

'You look beautiful,' the queen said tartly.

Mur cast her eyes down demurely.

'In the face of your own beauty everything else fails, Your Majesty,' she replied.

In spite of the grimness of the situation, Asandhimitra burst out laughing. 'You have a silver tongue, girl. It must bring you many golden opportunities.' She turned to Suma. 'You brought me news of a murder in Pataliputra,' she said. 'And now another has occurred in Ujjain. Does it not appear strange to you, ambassador?'

Suma's eyes opened wide. His mouth slackened.

'I hope the prin… er… the girl promised to our king is safe,' he inquired anxiously.

'I am afraid she has been killed,' Asandhimitra said. 'But have no doubt, my spymaster will discover the killer.'

'Considering the murder took place under his nose?' Suma blurted out.

Asandhimitra's eyes flashed.

'You go too far, ambassador,' she said sharply. 'You forget your place.'

Suma bit down his disappointment and apologized. Beads of sweat had appeared on his forehead, which he wiped away with a silk handkerchief. 'Your Majesty, I am a diplomat, not a spy. I wanted to take the girl to my king as a token of affection from you, she was so comely. Now how will I face him?' he moaned.

'We agree,' Asandhimitra said. 'But I smell a conspiracy. A murder inside my own palace! I am vexed.'

Suma bowed deeply. 'I hope this unfortunate event won't cast a shadow over your birthday celebrations,' he rallied. 'After all, the girl was just an orphan living on your kindness, as you say.'

'Everyone under my roof is under my protection, whether it be a concubine or a diplomat,' the queen said icily. 'Any harm done to them is harm intended for me.'

'I beg your indulgence, Your Majesty,' Suma protested. 'I did not mean to offend. I was merely pointing out that nothing should get in the way of your birthday celebrations.'

His voice verged on the thin side of insolence.

Lord Suma, curator of conspiracies and purveyor of political poison was a smooth operator, the Brahmin thought.

Asandhimitra signalled for Suma to leave. He bowed himself out.

'What is he going to do now, I wonder,' she said thoughtfully when he had left.

'I have a plan,' the Brahmin said.

Outside the palace, a cool wind flowed down from the flanks of the mountains, skipping across the placid tides of the Shipra to flirt with the trees in the palace garden. It paused to embrace a blooming kovidara tree and left, gathering leaves. A watcher on a distant balcony smiled as a single kovidara descended slowly on the grass like the echo of an unforgiving curse.

A Plot of Strangers

Ujjain had woken up to the sound of trumpets and drums announcing Queen Asandhimitra's birth. The atmosphere was festive with the music of conches and thousands of temple bells as the people of the city prayed to the gods to bless Ashoka's queen. The king himself, busy with his invasion plans and therefore unable to attend, sent a pure white stallion bred from the bloodline of Alexander's favourite horse, Bucephalus, as a gift. Ashoka knew Asandhimitra loved to ride, often going on hunts in the forest, accompanied by her noblemen and bodyguards. She was an expert archer who refused to hunt tigers and wild boars from the safety of elephant back, and was much admired for her skill with the javelin.

'Today is the day of the hunter,' Asandhimitra thought, hoping the Brahmin would track down the murderer in their midst soon. From her balcony, she surveyed the city, with its gleaming girdle of the Shipra. She watched the passage of boats, heard the faint, distant splash of their oars; Greek galleys carrying wine and olive oil to Pataliputra and lighter, long-hulled dhows loaded with dates, frankincense and myrrh from southern Arabia. She sighed, imagining the freedom of travel – billowing sails embracing the wind on magnificently lonely journeys through unchartered oceans. She envied the sailors who felt the salty wind on their weather-beaten faces and slept under the stars of an unsullied cobalt vault. For a moment, she wished she was not a queen, trapped in intrigue, murder and war, but just a woman on a ship feeling the freedom of the wind on her face.

She set the thought aside. She was Ashoka's queen, and ruled the kingdom by his side. Soon she would be carried forth in bejewelled glory to the Shiva temple atop Ujjain's sacred hill. Large numbers of citizens had already gathered all along the barricaded roads to cheer her. A huge crowd, held at bay by armed soldiers, surrounded the large stone quadrangle of the palace. Steps led down from its terrace towards a waiting golden palanquin, surrounded by six muscular African slaves naked to the waist, wearing white loincloths. Two war elephants caparisoned in gold-coloured cloth studded with rubies, diamonds and amethysts stood on either side. A loud roar went up as Asandhimitra appeared with Iantha by her side. Framed by the gigantic door frame, she cut a graceful figure in a long white flowing dress; a golden circlet kept her dark, waist-length hair in place. Her gown was bunched below her breasts in the Greek fashion, leaving her arms bare.

From afar, the Brahmin watched her descend the steps, smiling and waving, showing no sign of the unease she must be feeling. His eyes scanned the crowd for the glint of a knife or the quick movement of an arbalest being pulled out from under a cloak.

Nothing.

Archers were strategically placed at every vantage point on the ramparts, terraces and rooftops, bows notched. He heaved a sigh of relief as the royal parade started without incident. People cheered and reached out as treasury officials flung fistfuls of gold and silver coins in the air.

As he joined the crowds, he wondered where Hao was. Had she returned from her mission?

As if she had read his mind, Hao suddenly appeared beside him.

'Is it done?' he asked.

She nodded.

The Brahmin smiled, relieved. She melted back into the crowd. He walked through the crowded streets, marvelling at the number of people who had come from all over the kingdom to celebrate the queen's birthday. Only the back alleys, which ran parallel to the houses and shops, were empty. Suddenly he caught sight of two cloaked figures engrossed in conversation in one such alley. Sensing his presence, they looked in his direction. One of them seemed familiar. He stepped back, looking for a way to divert their attention from him. A few metres away, a pair of old women were quarrelling over some coins they had managed to catch. The Brahmin signalled to a face in the crowd. A few moments later, an urchin darted out from behind the women, snatched the coins and ran back into the crowd. They started yelling, 'Thief, thief!' at the top of their voices. Unfortunately for the boy, a policeman patrolling nearby saw the incident and grabbed him by the scruff of his neck. The boy lashed out with his foot and received a heavy blow in return. He collapsed to the ground.

'He's going to lose his hand, or be thrown to the

crocodiles in the moat for assaulting a king's officer,' someone in the crowd ventured.

'Serves him right,' came the response.

The policeman cuffed the boy and dragged him to the nearest Pradesika Sthan – the building where his crime would be recorded before he was carted off to prison for sentencing by dharmasthiyas – judges presiding over the kanthakasodhanas, the criminal courts.

The spymaster fell into step beside the policeman.

'Take him to the station, but don't charge him. Give him food and water and keep him there until I arrive. On no account will you hurt him,' he warned.

The policeman turned around with a scowl. 'And who might you be to challenge the king's law…'

The Brahmin showed him the royal ring. The policeman's face paled.

'I'm sorry, your humble servant did not realize…' he spluttered.

The Brahmin patted him on the shoulder and told him not to worry.

'You were doing your duty and doing it well,' he said.

He thrust some coins into the policeman's hand. 'The boy is my spy. I wanted him to create a diversion,' he said.

'Something dangerous we should worry about?' the man asked, worried.

'Conspiracies in a kingdom as great as ours are common, as you know. But we're here to protect it, aren't we?'

The law keeper's face glowed with pride at being included in the Brahmin's activities. Before he could thank him, the spymaster had melted back into the crowd, moving swiftly towards the back alley where he had seen the two cloaked figures.

Hao was waiting for him there. A casual observer would have mistaken her for a traveller who had come to Ujjain to see the queen's procession.

'That was a good distraction,' she ventured.

'Isn't improvisation a spy's best weapon?' the Brahmin asked. 'Luckily I was able to spot one of our boys from the urchin brigade. Where are the two men who were here?'

'Alarmed by the commotion, they fled,' Hao said. 'But I followed them.'

'One of them looked like Suma,' the spymaster said.

'You're right. The evil Lord Suma in person. The other man was Telemachus.'

The Brahmin looked at her with a question in his eyes.

Hao continued, 'Since I was hiding on a ledge high above, I could hear only snatches of their conversation. They were speaking in whispers. I think maybe they saw you. They rushed towards the other end of the alley where their horses were. Suma rode away in the direction of the palace, and Telemachus to the forest.'

The Brahmin looked thoughtful.

'Aren't those trumpets that I hear? The queen must have returned from the temple. Let's go and meet her. There is much to discuss.'

Gifts from the Enemy

'The murder of the dancing girl has cast a shadow over the palace, especially the women and the servants,' Queen Asandhimitra told the Brahmin, sipping delicately from a silver goblet of Rhodes wine.

She had returned from her trip to the hilltop temple after receiving Lord Shiva's blessings. The Brahmin looked out through the high doorway of her chamber, towards a wide, open terrace protected by the queen's bodyguard – heavily muscled men with steely eyes and firm chins. A line of maidens-in-waiting dressed in sheer white silk, doe-eyed, red-lipped and fair-faced, clustered near the door, giggling and chattering and darting swift glances towards the queen's chamber. Two tall African warriors with wicked looking scimitars flanked the steps of a richly carpeted platform overlooking the palace courtyard. The Brahmin had suggested to Asandhimitra that she receive Suma's obeisance from there, forcing the envoy to look up towards her. The height would make him feel small, at a disadvantage. She noticed the direction of his glance and smiled.

'Impressive, don't you think?' she asked, indicating the assembly on the terrace.

She sat with her legs tucked under her on a kline, a rectangular Grecian couch. Asandhimitra, like so many highborn women in Magadha, favoured Greek furniture. The seat of the wooden couch, inlaid with ivory and tortoiseshell designs, was covered with a goose feather bed.

She gestured to the Brahmin to take his seat on a wooden klismos – a Greek chair with a curved back and legs.

'How is your plan going?' she asked. She looked calm, in spite of the murder in the palace.

'Our enemies, led by Lord Suma, have hatched a plot to destroy Magadha. At the centre of the conspiracy is a weapon of destruction, which everyone including the king seems to want.'

At the mention of the weapon, Asandhimitra's face suddenly became unreadable. The Brahmin realized a difficult conversation lay ahead.

'Who are these conspirators? Is the murderer of the girls one of them?' she asked.

The Brahmin shook his head regretfully.

'I am the king's master of secrets, my lady. If I have a reason to hide something, you must believe it is a sound one. I beg you to wait until tomorrow when all will be revealed. Meanwhile, I need you to put on another act.'

The queen's gaze softened. She said, 'Ashoka is right, you are a stubborn rascal. But I trust you and your reasons. What would you have me do?'

'The essential aspect of espionage is to defeat one conspiracy with another. I need you to be part of my conspiracy.'

'How exciting,' she said drily. 'Next, you will ask me to be one of your spies.'

The Brahmin continued undeterred, 'Today, Lord Suma will arrive in the city with his mysterious gift. But it is a dangerous gift.'

She raised a sceptical eyebrow. The Brahmin went on, 'For my plan to succeed and for Suma to be exposed, you must act pleased with his gift and express your appreciation by bestowing the Order of the Golden Lion on him.'

'Have you gone mad, Brahmin? The Golden Lion is Magadha's greatest honour. Suma wishes to see us destroyed. And I don't trust that Mur at all, with her eastern eyes and vishakanya lips. I am convinced she is a poison maiden herself. Trust the great Chanakya to think of such devious methods to murder people.'

'Vishakanyas were not Chanakya's idea, Your Majesty,' the Brahmin replied. 'The Nandas sent one such woman to kill King Chandragupta, but Chanakya bribed her to seduce King Parvatak of Himavat, Nanda's ally, instead. I don't think Mur is a vishakanya. She may have poison in her heart, but her weapons are different.'

'Her weapons are beauty and treachery. I suspect she is behind Devavarman's murder and the theft of the war plans.'

'We shall find out soon enough. Everything has a price, Your Majesty. To be paid either in silver or in blood. Devavarman paid with his blood.'

'Devavarman was supposed to be loyal to his king.'

'I don't trust loyalty. It can be bought if the price is right. Like Suma, who is, for now, loyal to his general and his king.'

At the mention of the Kalingan's name, Asandhimitra's face darkened.

'And you tell me to honour this treacherous man with the Order of the Golden Lion.'

'Sometimes honours have to be wasted for a greater purpose. This is one such time.'

'Is that all you want from me?'

'No. Afterwards, I need you to hold a great banquet as a sign of peace between Kalinga and Magadha. It must start in the evening and go on until dawn.'

'For peace?' The queen laughed harshly. 'You think my words will deceive Suma at a time when the king is preparing for war?'

'Deception is the soul of espionage, my queen. You can't deceive your enemy with words, but you can sow the seeds of confusion in his heart with your actions. A confused enemy is a weak enemy.'

The queen nodded doubtfully.

'Anything else?' she asked.

'Yes. Arrange a separate feast for the garrison guards. They must gorge on so much food and wine that they will be rendered useless. Only a small contingent will be left to guard the palace and the city.'

'You are insane, spymaster. If all my soldiers are drunk, who will guard us?'

'You do not need to worry on that account, my queen. Alternative arrangements will be in place.'

With a sigh, Asandhimitra slumped further in her seat.

'I am trusting my life and my city to you and your crazy ideas. And you will not reveal a thing.'

'I am trusting you to safeguard the interests of Magadha by trusting me,' the spymaster said gravely.

'If something untoward happens here, which I am sure it could with Suma around, the king will have your head.'

'The king is on his way here, my lady. I have sent word to him.'

'Ashoka? Coming here? Why was I not told?'

'Had you known, you would have thrown the city into a tizzy, ordering copious amounts of wine, fowl and meat for a welcome feast. Your officials would have plundered the bazaar, purchasing heaps of flowers and masses of drapery to decorate the palace; sweets for children and silver coins to distribute to the poor. There are more Kalingan spies in Ujjain than flies in a butcher's shop. They would have alerted Suma immediately and he would have guessed the king's arrival.'

'Surely he would not dare harm Ashoka,' she snarled.

'A game of life and death is being played here, my queen,' he answered. 'Kalinga will stop at nothing to prevent war. With the king out of the way, they could invade us first and take Magadha.'

Drums sounded outside, faint and distant at first, but growing louder and closer with each beat. The Brahmin went across to the window, parted the damask curtains and looked out. 'Suma's mysterious gift is here, on its way to the palace,' he remarked.

Asandhimitra looked out of the window and gasped. 'It's gigantic,' she said. 'See how it gleams. It's indeed as grand as Suma promised.'

The Brahmin's face bore a serious expression as he watched the procession approaching the palace along the wide road that led to the city gates. Word had spread about Suma's gift. A massive crowd filled the palace courtyard. At the head of the procession rode Lord Suma and Mur on two white steeds. Behind them came the drummers whose rhythmic beats tattooed the morning. A team of sixteen white bullocks followed, dragging a massive gold-and-silver sculpture of an elephant, over twenty feet high, mounted on a polished mahogany platform on wheels. It was protected by a contingent of soldiers in the unmistakable Kalingan uniform, bearing lances flying the flag of the boy-king Srutayush. A long line of silver palanquins swathed in costly silks, decorated with pink and white lotuses, brought up the rear. The Brahmin counted one hundred of them. He wondered why there was no cavalry to protect them.

The procession was a spectacular sight: the gigantic elephant figure glistening in the soft sun, its saluting trunk spewing out a small fountain, which fell into a silver basin concealing a cunning arrangement of pipes and bellows to keep the water in circulation. Its eyes glittered with rubies the size of small rocks. Carvings on its sides depicted a queen hunting in a forest teeming with deer and wild boar. Birds sang from fruit-laden branches. Bejewelled flowers bloomed brilliantly. On the elephant's forehead was carved Ashoka's lion symbol. On its back sat a resplendent howdah, covered with golden gauze and ruched purple silk with silver trimmings. Bars of pure gold protected its sides. A tall golden throne was installed on it. A shining red silken umbrella, bordered with gold brocade, was positioned behind the seat upon a golden rod. Steps cut into the sides led up to the howdah.

Asandhimitra clapped her hands in excitement.

'A gold-and-silver elephant! A present fit for a queen indeed!' she exclaimed, her unease forgotten.

'It is also a gift of death, Your Majesty,' the Brahmin whispered.

In a few words, he explained to Asandhimitra the true purpose behind the gift. He told her in detail about Hao's discovery on her mission to the forest. Fear and anger darkened the queen's eyes.

The Brahmin said comfortingly, 'Nothing will happen to you, I promise, my queen. You will leave the banquet in the middle, for a safe place. Hao will take you. Until then you must keep calm.'

As if on cue, the Viet spy entered the chamber. Asandhimitra searched her face for any sign of fear. There was none.

'It is time for the first act of our play, Your Majesty,' the Brahmin said.

The queen nodded, stepped out to the terrace and waved to the crowd below. They cheered loudly and waved back. The city was out on the streets, eager to see the queen's birthday gift. A long line of soldiers held the crowds back with locked spears. Archers lined the walls, bows and arrows notched. It was the first time that a detachment of Kalingan soldiers, however small, was entering Ujjain; the commander of the guard did not wish to take any chances.

Suma's procession reached the palace gates. A broad smile was visible on his face as the group entered the complex, making for the palace courtyard. The Brahmin glimpsed armour behind the soldiers' tabards. Swords swung from studded leather waist-belts. Sharpened lances glistened in the light of the day.

'How dare they bring weapons into the palace grounds?' Asandhimitra said angrily. They stood watching as Suma ordered the drummers to stop. The bullocks heaved, and the elephant glided forward on its wheeled platform and came to a stop below Asandhimitra. At a barked command from the captain of the contingent, lances were lowered in a gesture of submission. The palanquins were gently placed on the ground. Suma and Mur got off their horses and bowed.

Suma looked up at the queen, anxious to read her response. Asandhimitra's face was impassive. A great silence fell on the courtyard. The crowd was waiting for their queen to respond.

Suddenly she gave a radiant smile and clapped. The crowd broke into loud cheers. Suma wiped his forehead. Mur was smiling too, though her eyes were alert, as though searching for someone. The Brahmin stood unseen in the doorway's shadow as, with a graceful gesture, Asandhimitra invited Suma to come inside.

Suma entered the formal visiting hall, his eyes narrowing at the sight of the Brahmin and Hao. But his smile was crafty.

'I hope you like our humble gift,' he murmured to Asandhimitra in a servile tone.

'It's magnificent,' she replied. 'We are pleased indeed. You must join our traditional birthday banquet as honoured guests.'

'Thank you, Your Majesty. It is a great privilege to be invited to your banquet. I hope your birthday ride next year will be on our elephant.'

Asandhimitra inclined her head gracefully.

'We have brought more gifts, Your Majesty,' Suma continued. 'Our king has personally handpicked one hundred virgins from Kalinga, each fairer than the other, to be your maids of honour. They are all trained in music, dance, conversation and the art of arranging flowers.'

Asandhimitra nodded her thanks.

'I am so pleased with your gifts that I want to share my happiness with my people. I shall declare today a holiday for the city and my soldiers.'

She tuned to a courtier.

'Prepare a great feast for all the soldiers and guards. Let them eat and drink their fill. Let us celebrate, for we are with trusted friends now.'

The Brahmin did not miss the surprised glance Suma gave Mur. This was going even better than planned, her look seemed to say in response.

'You are most generous, Your Majesty,' Suma said. 'There are few queens who bestow such kindness on ordinary soldiers. I am sure it will be a pleasant surprise for them.'

'Send the Kalingan girls to the Chamber of the Virgins,' Asandhimitra ordered, turning again to the courtier who stood beside her. 'I shall inspect them later.'

He curtsied and hurried away.

The Brahmin whispered in Hao's ear and she left the room quickly. The Brahmin noticed Suma's eyes cloud with suspicion at her departure and smiled to himself. As the long line of palanquins proceeded towards their destination inside the palace, the sun began its slide from its zenith, heralding the darkness to follow.

The Spy's Escape

The Brahmin and Hao left the royal visiting hall and slipped into the winter afternoon's mellow light. Guards snapped to attention as they passed along the long corridor around the main building. Preparations for the feast were in full swing. Troupes of dancers from the faraway Pandya and Chola empires in the south were practicing their steps – dusky, voluptuous beauties enveloped in the scent of jasmine, silver anklets laughing as they spun to the frenzied beat of drums and the snaking tunes of flutes. Conjurers practiced their tricks, blowing plumes of fire as they wriggled and wheeled around on tall, brightly painted poles. A few dwarves in red loincloths wrestled inside a small ring, pushing and heaving in the mud, watched by laughing people. A group of soldiers watched two young boys engaged in a mock swordfight, cheering and whistling at every blow. Festivities inside the main palace would be more refined.

He suddenly felt Hao's presence, as she fell into step with him. His face darkened hearing what Hao had to tell him. As they strolled beneath the painted ceiling of the corridor deep in thought, they could hear the chiming of bells. Unseen dancers stamped their feet to the tune of 'tha-ka dhi-mi tha-ki-ta…'

'Bharatanatyam and Karnatic music being performed in Magadha?' the Brahmin mused. 'The Tamil empires must be taking Ashoka seriously.'

'These performers must be bound for Pataliputra, they probably stopped for the banquet,' said Hao. 'War is good for business, that's when dancers and courtesans are at their busiest. They help the great lords to take their minds away from death.'

News of the impending war had spread far and wide. The Brahmin wondered how many among the entertainers were spies.

The distinctive sound of a drum being played with one hand came to him, accompanied by a soft voice singing in a familiar language. He stopped to listen.

'A devotional song in Pali?' he wondered aloud. 'It's rare to hear the language of Kalinga being spoken inside a Magadhan palace. Let's see what's going on in that hall, Hao.'

They entered the the big airy room with large arched windows and a domed ceiling.

The sight of a familiar form holding a dance pose greeted them; her body bent in three places in the shape of a helix, eyes closed in rapture, a soft smile upon her painted lips. Her torso swayed like a richly adorned serpent. She wore a silver mahkoot – a dancer's crown with a floral back piece or 'gobha' adorning her hair, gathered into a bun at the nape of her neck. From a filigreed silver headpiece hung a silver lotus glittering with diamonds. Little umbrella-shaped earrings adorned her delicate ears. She wore a necklace around her lithe neck and a longer one sporting a boar pendent, the royal emblem of Kalinga, swayed on her small, firm breasts. The silver bangles on her upper arms and wrists clinked as she moved. Tiny bells sewn into padded anklets tinkled melodiously as her feet met the floor slowly but forcefully.

'An excellent tribhangi,' the Brahmin applauded her.

Mur stopped dancing. She opened her kohl-thickened eyes and her gaze locked with his.

'I didn't know you could dance,' the Brahmin said. 'And dance so well.'

'There are many things I do well, spymaster,' she said in a deceptively beguiling voice. 'Tonight is Kalinga's night and I plan to give a special performance for your queen.'

The spymaster bowed graciously.

'Do continue dancing. I look forward to watching you later in the evening,' he said, turning on his heel with Hao behind him.

The palace was busy with arrangements for the feast. They passed lines of palace lackeys carrying huge rolls of Persian carpets on their shoulders. Others hurried behind them with fat silk cushions and bolsters. Servants passed to and fro with gold plates, goblets and cutlery. They inspected the huge banquet hall, where carpenters were busy constructing a low platform in the centre for the singers and dancers.

'We might as well get something to eat and rest a while,' the Brahmin told his assistant, satisfied at the progress of the preparations. 'We have a busy night ahead.'

He stopped a palace official who was on his way to an office in the administrative section of the palace, accompanied by his clerks.

'Well?' said the man arrogantly. 'Can't you see I'm busy? I'm going about the queen's business.'

'Even those who are on the queen's business need to eat,' the Brahmin responded laconically, running his eyes over the official's corpulent person. 'If you would be kind enough to guide me to the nearest dining hall, I would consider it a favour.'

The man's face reddened with anger. He puffed his pigeon chest out.

'Who are you to ask me that?' he demanded angrily, his piggy eyes taking in the Brahmin's simple cotton tabard worn over a black linen undershirt; crimson leggings thrust into black leather boots and the heavy sword snug in its scabbard on a thick leather baldric around muscled shoulders. Then he glared at Hao. His clerks tittered excitedly, the prospect of trouble promising a break in the monotony of their day.

'A common mercenary with his whore, stopping an important palace official,' one of them snapped. 'Don't you know carrying weapons inside the palace is forbidden unless you are a royally appointed guard?'

His master nodded self-importantly. He turned and clapped his pudgy hands, calling out to the nearest guard.

'Arrest them!' he said, pointing at the two spies. The guard stepped forward, then stopped abruptly. The Brahmin's hand had strayed towards his sword and Ashoka's ring shone on his finger, like a red star. The clerks stopped their malicious mutterings, sudden panic rising in their eyes. The sight of the ring had transfixed the palace official, too. He slumped to the floor at the Brahmin's feet, begging for mercy.

'Forgive me, master, I didn't know you are the king's man,' he wailed. 'I'm just a petty official, please don't punish me.'

Hao burst out laughing. The Brahmin moved his leg away from the man's clasp distastefully.

'We're hungry, and don't have much time. Show me to the dining hall and be off,' he said brusquely.

The official and his clerks led them bowing and scraping to one of the many dining rooms in the palace complex. As they entered, sunlight streamed in through the radius windows, temporarily dazzling them. But the Brahmin did not miss the cloaked man at a corner table, who abruptly rose and left the room, his meal unfinished. Hao tried to follow, but he had already slipped into the crowds loitering in the courtyard, waiting for the queen's birthday feast to start. The Brahmin turned to the official and his men and barked, 'Did you see that man?'

They shook their heads in dumb fear. This tall, dark, lean-limbed stranger, with his piercing eyes and cruel mouth, terrified them. The woman scared them even more, for in spite of her beauty, it was as if death accompanied her, disguised as her shadow.

The Brahmin spat in disgust and waved them away.

'He looked familiar but the sun was in my eyes,' he said to Hao, once they had sat down at a nearby table and called for food and wine.

'Telemachus?' Hao asked, raising her tumbler to her mouth.

'Perhaps. Mind his infernal cheek, dining openly in palace halls when he knows he will be killed by my men if he is recognized.'

'He is tricky, for he spies for Suma.'

'I'm glad he does. What he sees and hears here will only make him more confident that Suma's plans will succeed.'

People were milling about in the courtyard, examining the stalls selling fragrances made from dried spices and flowers, wooden toys and bales of coloured cloth.

The cloaked man walked among the crowds, giving thanks to his god that the Brahmin had not recognized him.

Or had he?

A group of cavalry clattered by, leaving behind the whiff of horse sweat and leather. One of the horses trod in a puddle, splashing water on his cloak. He swore viciously. The cavalryman turned around scowling, and he quickly averted his face, pulling the hood of his cloak over it. As he walked among the crowds, listening to their excited chatter about the feast, the queen and the gold-and-silver elephant, the last of his doubts disappeared. Tonight was going to be the night of change.

He pledged he would make an offering to Athena, the goddess of war tomorrow, once all the meticulous planning of over a year had borne fruit.

Feast of Fear

Asandhimitra's palace blazed with lights. The night lapped around the edges of Ujjain, like a shape shifter kept at bay by the spell of a powerful magus. From the balcony of his room, the Brahmin watched the dusk give way to the brightness of thousands of lamps and torches. The mellow melody of a musician tuning his harp came from somewhere within the palace. Far away, little lights flickered here and there on the furry slopes of the low hills – Buddhist monks getting ready for their prayers in their caves. Temple bells sang in the wind, their music swimming around the palace. The oval stone in the temple of Harsiddhi Devi outside the courtyard was smeared with fresh vermillion, like the shaven head of a novice priest. The city's great wooden gates were wide open.

The Brahmin watched the citizens of Ujjain streaming in – men, women and children, in colourful clothes, laughing and chattering about the festivities that awaited them. He noticed that there were only two sentries each – a lookout and an archer – to man the tall watchtowers on the walls. It would take some hours for their replacements to arrive since the feast would be a raucous affair. Even then, the guards would be too drunk and well-fed to respond swiftly or effectively to an enemy attack. It would take only a small army to capture the palace.

The spymaster smiled grimly, listening to the noisy sounds of soldiers in the barracks making merry.

In the centre of the courtyard stood the gold-and-silver elephant, glowing in silent majesty. A large crowd surrounded it, gazing in awe and discussing its grandeur. Many praised the power of Magadha, which had made Kalinga offer such a magnificent gift to the queen. A tight circle of Kalingan solders in full armour guarded it, their spears thrust forward to prevent anyone from getting close. Even the few children who escaped the clasp of their parents to examine it were roughly shooed away.

The Brahmin surveyed the scene carefully. His gaze passed over the barracks and guardhouses, calculating their distance from the main building. A lone war elephant trumpeted from its stables at the far end of the palace. The Brahmin had seen them in action in many battles he had fought with Ashoka. His blood raced at the memory of the fearsome, armoured beasts with iron spikes on their trunks trumpeting with bloodlust as they ploughed through foot soldiers and cavalry, swatting aside chariots as archers in leather howdas loosened clouds of arrows on the enemy. The Brahmin wondered how many battles this lone elephant had fought in.

On the western side of the palace wall, war chariots lay tilted, their polished wheel blades glinting cruelly. Warriors from Uttarapatha – Kambojas, Yavanas, Sakas, and a platoon of Naga soldiers – marched towards the dining space behind the garrison. A group of dancing girls in gaudy finery, accompanied by singers, flautists and drummers, crossed their path. A soldier made a lewd remark at which his companions laughed uproariously. One of the girls flicked her long braid at him like a whip. As he laughingly tried to grab her, she stepped back with swift grace; her anklets chimed as she ran to catch up with her companions.

In spite of the grimness of the situation, the Brahmin smiled at the sight. He made his way up the long curving flight of steps towards the terrace that ran all the way around the royal dining hall. He knew each and every part of the palace, every secret door and passage, the blind alleys and prison rooms where a person could be locked away and forgotten forever.

The Brahmin entered the queen's dining hall. At the opposite ends of a long table that could easily seat a hundred guests stood two tall golden chairs with the royal lion of Magadha carved in relief on their head pieces. The taller of the two chairs, at the head of the table, was Ashoka's, which now stood unoccupied. When the queen held a feast in the king's absence, the empty chair opposite her reminded everyone that Ashoka's looming presence pervaded the room. Behind the each royal chair stood two huge Macedonian soldiers in armour, holding thick, long spears. Falcatas – the deadliest of the swords used by the Greek army – were stuck into their belts. Their inward curving blades could deliver blows strong enough to break shields and helmets. One of the guards looked familiar, a grizzled old warrior, and the Brahmin nodded at him but got no response.

Suddenly three trumpet notes sounded, accompanied by drumbeats and cymbals. Asandhimitra walked in smiling, wearing a white linen chiton pinned at the shoulder with a gold peacock brooch. A string of shining white pearls from Lanka adorned her long, slender neck. Her high cheekbones were lightly painted, her face lightly powdered. Her lustrous black eyes looked even larger with kohl. Her lips, painted carmine, curved upward in a regal smile. A murmur of admiration ran through the room. Asandhimitra clapped her hands and gestured for the guests to take their places.

'This birthday banquet is also in Lord Suma's honour, in appreciation of his magnificent gift,' she announced.

The Brahmin watched the Kalingan ambassador bow to the queen with exaggerated flourish.

'The honour belongs to Kalinga, whose gift is a symbol of the love that binds our great kingdoms,' he declared in his low sibilant voice.

'Indeed it is, isn't it?' she said.

She turned and clapped her hands. An attendant came in bearing a gold lion on a gold salver.

'The Order of the Golden Lion,' Asandhimitra declared. 'Hereby I bestow Magadha's greatest honour on you, Lord Suma.'

The ambassador was overwhelmed. Even Mur looked taken aback. The audience was surprised into silence. Such a rare honour from the queen meant that Ashoka held Suma in high esteem. All talk of war between the two countries were just rumours then, they surmised and sighed with relief. Suma went down on one knee and accepted the award with a bowed head. The Brahmin could see that he was genuinely moved.

'I thank you for your benevolence, Your Majesty,' he whispered hoarsely.

Asandhimitra smiled. The moment was over. She gestured to the assemblage to sit back and enjoy the feast. A multitude of palace attendants streamed in with silver trays of steaming white long-grained rice, fragrant with cardamoms and cinnamon, sprinkled with fried cashewnuts from the south and buttoned with sultanas from Persia. Quail stuffed with thinly sliced boiled eggs swimming in rich gravy, roast legs of venison, capon filled with spiced minced lamb and bowls of freshly cooked vegetables were passed around. Liveried helpers stood behind the guests, continuously replenishing their plates and goblets with food and wine. People ate, drank and groaned with pleasure. On the platform for the performances, a turbaned singer in a spotless white tunic sang of the flight of swans and the longing of nightingales. The queen picked at her food, refusing wine, her eyes gazing into some distant world only she could see. The chair beside Suma stood empty, and the Brahmin wondered where Mur was. Suddenly Suma stood up to applaud a dancer who had made a dramatic entrance with small delicate steps, the bells on her anklets tinkling in silvery rhythm. A fleeting moment of confusion furrowed Asandhimitra's perfectly painted eyebrows. Then she clapped loudly. The assembled guests stopped eating and began to clap too, though none of them understood why she was greeting the dancer so enthusiastically.

'Mur, we are delighted,' Asandhimitra exclaimed.

'How lovely you look. It appears that Kalinga is full of surprises today.'

Mur bowed graciously, her eyes fixed on Asandhimitra's smiling face. Her full red lips parted in a small smile. She was dressed in the rich elaborate costume of dancers from the eastern lands – a nine-yard vermillion silk garment covered her curvaceous body, her red kanchula blouse sparkled with tiny diamonds and her shapely legs were covered with a red-silk frilled nibibhanda. She wore a headpiece of white jasmine flowers, which contrasted with her lustrous long black hair, coiled in the shape of a flower behind her neck. As the first drum beat began, and the soft notes of a Pali love song rose into the silence, Mur began to dance with slow, graceful movements, accelerating her tempo gradually until her dark eyes, swan-like neck, shimmering silky body and silver anklets became a single blazing entity of colour, shape and sound. Her hands moved with grace and speed, tracing elaborate patterns in the air. When she finished her dance to thunderous applause, Suma, his face glowing with pride, clapped the loudest. He turned to the queen with a wide smile, anticipating her appreciation.

Asandhimitra was gone.

Virgins of Death

Hao hurried Asandhimitra along an underground corridor accessed through a hidden trapdoor in Ashoka's bedroom, which the queen had not been aware of. Upon reaching a point where the corridor turned right, she paused to examine the wall. She pressed a brick laid at shoulder height, the slight difference in colour visible only to the trained eye. A section of the wall moved silently to the side, revealing a passageway into a large airy room. It was a secret chamber situated above the garrison, cunningly hidden by a latticed red stone screen. Through a curtain of rose bushes and hydrangea vines, Asandhimitra and Hao could observe the feast below. It seemed to be a success, judging by the bawdy songs of the soldiers and the happy laughter of the dancing girls.

'You are safe here, nobody knows of this place except the Brahmin and the king,' Hao said.

'I thought by now Ashoka would have shown me all the secret places in this palace,' Asandhimitra said ruefully. 'But then kings love secrets, even when they love you.'

'My master told me the king built this room for you if your life were ever in danger.'

Asandhimitra sighed – a mixture of affection and exasperation. Hao went up to a sideboard and poured wine into a goblet for the queen.

'I have to leave now. You must not open the door to anyone, except me or my master. Do not let anybody in, especially not Lord Suma or Mur.'

'Where will you be?' Asandhimitra asked, a faint trace of worry in her voice.

'I'm going to end what they started,' Hao replied. 'I'll be back soon.'

Asandhimitra nodded, her composure regained.

'A piece of advice, my lady,' Hao said. 'Please do not use the peephole, ever. A needle-knife pushed through it into your eye will reach your brain and kill you instantaneously.'

Asandhimitra shuddered at the thought.

'I won't,' she said.

Hao slipped out of the secret room and went looking for the Brahmin. She found him standing in the shadow of a watchtower, surveying the courtyard anxiously. Even the last tiny sliver of moon had vanished. The night sky looked as if it had been washed with thick black ink. The torchlights in the palace flickered without enthusiasm, unable to keep the darkness away; the oil in their basins was almost finished. The soldiers and attendants were too busy fornicating with the whores and dancing girls or just too drunk, the Brahmin guessed. A tiny cold wind tiptoed on his skin. He shivered and muttered a prayer, which came clumsily to his lips since he hardly ever sought the gods' intervention.

The great gold-and-silver elephant in the courtyard looked like an eerie phantom from some ancient legend. The Brahmin saw a figure stepping out from the thick shadows between the heavy pillars of a portico in a far corner. It looked around furtively to check if anyone was watching. Satisfied, it ran towards the elephant.

'You are in a tearing hurry,' the Kalingan guard's voice carried across in the wind as he stepped aside to let the figure pass.

It roughly pushed the guard aside and scrambled up the steps to the howdah, gripped the platform with both hands and pushed. The howda slid aside noiselessly. The climber gave a low whistle. An answering whistle came from inside.

'Hecuba! It begins now,' the Brahmin whispered.

Hecuba, the queen of Troy – a city deceived by the Trojan horse. Was Asandhimitra, the queen of Magadha, to be deceived by a trick elephant that hid a hundred men? Another trap prepared by Suma's guileful mind?

'Didn't I tell you it would be a Trojan elephant?' Hao whispered, reappearing beside him. 'Suma is clever. But not as clever as us.'

But who had sent the warning about Hecuba? That was still a mystery.

The Brahmin waited for the drama to unfold. Suddenly an arrow flew out of nowhere and struck the cloaked figure on the elephant. It teetered in the air and fell back with a cry. The Brahmin heaved a sigh of relief.

Hao had fulfilled her mission. Angyo had arrived as promised.

As soon as the Viet girl had come to him with news of the Kalingan soldiers and the elephant hidden inside the forest, he had ordered her to ride to Tamralipti to ask for Angyo's help. It had come at a price, but one he was only too glad to pay.

A horde of warrior monks led by Angyo burst into

the square now, shooting at the Kalingan soldiers guarding the elephant figure. Caught by surprise, their bodies were ripped apart by the hail of arrows. The Brahmin quickly ordered Hao back into the palace to protect the queen, for Suma could not be underestimated. Then he yelled to Angyo, 'After me!'

The fighter monk smoothly slipped off the saddle of his piebald and ran after him. The Brahmin had already reached the top of the elephant when Angyo caught up, just in time to see grappling hooks attached to rope ladders being thrown up from inside. A large contingent of armed Kalingan soldiers, who had been hiding there, jostled to ascend the ladders, alerted by the cries of their fallen comrades. What followed was a massacre. With jaw-dropping skill, Angyo's archers rained down arrows through the opening upon the trapped men. A team of warrior monks had rapidly climbed up to where the Brahmin and Angyo stood. Together, they hacked down any surviving soldiers who reached the top rungs in a desperate attempt to fight or die. The screams of the wounded and dying rose from inside. Blood flowed through the cracks and joints of the wooden belly of the beast.

When the defenders climbed down to the courtyard, it was slippery with blood. The dead guards lay in grotesque postures. Arrows sprouted from their faces, necks, backs, chests and limbs. The mounted monks gazed down expressionlessly at the carnage they had wrought, their crimson cloaks pulled back to reveal the glinting hilts of their swords. They were big men all, not one of them under six feet.

Amid the heap of the dead men lay a cloaked figure, the shaft of an arrow protruding from his chest. His eyes stared at the heavens, as if dismayed at the sight of his fleeing shade.

'Telemachus, as I thought,' the Brahmin said. 'Suma has failed again.'

The first notes of the midnight bugle began to rise from a distant watchtower.

'Hurry, that's their signal, there's no time to lose! Off to the Chamber of the Virgins,' he yelled to Angyo, drawing his sword. As they thundered into the palace, followed by the monks, the sentries at the doors grouped into fighting formation. Seeing the Brahmin, they stopped.

'Don't move from your positions, and kill anyone who tries to get past you, man or woman,' he shouted as he ran.

The Brahmin and the warriors from Tamralipti moved swiftly along the heavily guarded corridors, repeating the warning to the guards they passed on the way. Sensing Angyo's puzzlement, he quickly appraised him of the real extent of Suma's plot. They rounded the last corner of the corridor, which led to the Chamber of the Virgins.

The guards whom Hao had posted there stood ready for his word.

'Open the doors,' he commanded. 'We've demolished the threat from outside, now to destroy the threat inside.'

At that very instant, they heard heavy pounding on the doors from within. With a great crash, the doors collapsed, flinging the guards aside. A mass of women in black rushed out with raised swords. Their heads were bound with black turbans, their breasts with black cloth. Dark leather strips covered their legs and feet. Their bodies glistened with oil.

They dispatched the stunned guards in the space of a few moments and rushed at the Brahmin and Angyo. The sight would have terrified even a hardened soldier. But Angyo's monks calmly let loose volley after volley of arrows at the attacking women, stepping back steadily to keep the distance between them and their targets. The first ranks teetered and fell. The rest, leaping over their fallen comrades, kept coming. The fight was fierce, neither side giving quarter. A monk fell, taking three women with him. The Brahmin and Angyo, standing side by side, parried, lunged and hacked with their heavy swords, thrusting their blades into soft bodies, ripping aside leather bindings and cutting open supple flesh. Even in the midst of the battle, the Brahmin felt reluctant admiration for the women.

In the end, they were all overwhelmed and killed.

'Who are these women?' a monk asked, sounding astonished. 'They fight like tigresses from hell.'

'They're not women, they are hermaphrodites,' the Brahmin answered. 'They are the best of Nandidevi's elite guard. It was his last desperate gamble, aided by Suma and his pet assassin, Mur.'

It was by a stroke of luck that Hao had discovered Suma's trickery. The cautious spy had decided to check the palanquins, all hundred of them, and accidentally glimpsed a hand parting a curtain. Its owner had raised a pair of wide, kohl-darkened eyes at Hao, letting an inviting giggle escape her painted mouth as she pulled the curtains together. But Hao had already noticed the strong, calloused fingers, and recognized a fighter's hand. Her alert brain signalled danger. Surreptitiously, she probed the palanquin's padded, silk-covered sides and cushions as it passed her. Her sensitive fingers felt the slight bulge made by the hilts of swords and daggers, concealed in the cotton stuffing. The women inside the palanquins relaxed at the sight of Hao's courteous, sometimes admiring smile as she parted curtain after curtain to reveal strikingly beautiful faces, one after the other. Just before the last one passed through the door into the Chamber of the Virgins, Hao ordered the guards to detain it and take its occupant to the torture chamber. In a few hours, she had all she needed to know.

War was suddenly in the air. The acrid smell of battle sweat and the coppery taste of blood on the floors rose to meet the sharp wind as it abseiled down the ridges from the mountain spurs, riding the flanks of the heavily wooded slopes with the force of an invading army.

The Brahmin put his arm around Angyo and squeezed. 'Thank you for your help, brother,' he said.

'What are brothers for? But I trust you haven't forgotten our pact?'

The spymaster nodded. The sky was beginning to lighten. It had been a long night. Just then, he heard the trilling of a nightjar from the direction of the palace gardens. It was repeated thrice. He raised his head and answered with the harsh cry of a hawk.

'That's our signal! Let's go,' he said, turning to Angyo. 'I need a couple of your monks.'

Angyo murmured an order. Two young warrior monks stepped forward.

'Go with him,' Angyo commanded. 'You are his until he tells you otherwise.'

'I'll need a horse,' the Brahmin said.

Angyo laughed and pointed at the gigantic gold-and-silver elephant and the corpses piled at its feet.

'Are you sure you don't need an elephant?' he joked.

A horse was quickly brought forward. The Brahmin swung a leg over its saddle and rode away with the two monks.

They reached the palace gate in time to see Hao blocking the way of two cloaked figures he recognized as Suma and Mur. The blade of her sword rested in the hollow of Suma's throat. A coach harnessed to two black horses stood beside them.

The Brahmin dismounted.

'So, what do we have here?' he remarked, walking up.

'You're addressing the envoy of Kalinga,' Suma blustered. 'Mind your tone.'

The Brahmin shrugged.

'There are many things we have addressed in the past hour – from a fake elephant to a hundred virgins. And what virgins they turned out to be! Sadly, they are all dead. Except one in a torture chamber.'

Suma's face blanched.

'Telemachus is responsible for this villainy,' he grovelled. 'We were looking all over the palace to warn you.'

'Is that so, my Lord?' the Brahmin asked. 'What villainy are you speaking of?'

Suma gulped.

'Your game is over, Suma. Both yours and Radhagupta's,' the Brahmin said. 'Did you think it would be so easy, to take the queen prisoner? I know your intention was to interrogate Her Majesty about the princess and the location of the Golden Scythe. Maybe with her help,' he said, pointing at Mur.

Her eyes blazed with hatred and malice.

The Brahmin continued, 'Once you had the Scythe, they would have been killed, I suppose, and you would have escaped to Kalingapatanam. Perhaps Radhagupta would have told Ashoka I was responsible, and that would have been the end of me. Kalinga would then attack Magadha, and with the Scythe, it would be invincible. Afterwards, Radhagupta would have been made king, no doubt.'

'But where is this Golden Scythe, if your theory is correct?' Suma sneered.

'Maybe you should ask the king of Lanka,' the Brahmin answered.

Suma's expression was suddenly anxious.

'You have lost, Suma. It was well played, but in this game of mirrors called espionage, only one can win. You are not to leave Magadha. Hao and these gentle monks will ensure you stay in your quarters until you're summoned by the king.'

'In the name of diplomacy, let me go. You have got what you wanted. The king is in Pataliputra, busy with plans of his own. I'm sure he is too busy to interrogate an insignificant creature like me,' Suma said ingratiatingly.

'Is he?' the Brahmin asked superciliously.

As if on cue, the sound of approaching thunder shook the palace grounds. Suma and Mur swung their gaze past him. The envoy's jaw dropped. Mur was transfixed to her spot. Even the monks looked alarmed. Their hands had gone to their weapons.

They saw a great storm sweeping towards the palace – a tossing forest of flashing spearheads and crimson pennants, each one emblazoned with a golden lion. The beat of thousands of hooves and the rhythmic marching of uncountable sandalled feet moving forward implacably to the steady beat of war drums shook the air. At the head of a great advancing army rode a dark figure clad in gleaming armour. Even from this distance, the Brahmin imagined he could discern the battle gleam in the cruel eyes and the twist of the unforgiving mouth in a face hewn from granite and obsidian.

Ashoka was coming to Ujjain for his queen.

The Brahmin Explains

'Let me tell you a story,' said the Brahmin, meeting the king's eyes without flinching. 'It's a story about power, greed, loyalty and compassion.'

Ashoka sat motionless on his serpent throne, his stony gaze fixed on the spymaster. His mouth was twisted between a smile and a snarl. His long black hair fell below his shoulders in thick braids, his neck strong and sinewy. Above his crowned head reared the bejewelled hood of his throne. A throne fit for a mighty king. Perhaps even for an emperor.

Next to Ashoka, on the dais covered with beautiful Persian carpets, sat Asandhimitra, whose slender grace contrasted with the king's looming presence. The Brahmin sensed the eagerness behind her serene exterior.

'This had better be good,' Ashoka growled. 'You dragged me from Pataliputra where I was busy with matters of state. You even insisted on a public audience, with the entire court present. Now, begin.'

The Brahmin's gaze gave nothing away. He bowed, allowing himself a smile so slight that it would have been missed, had Ashoka not been observing him closely.

'If it were anyone else, I would have executed him on the spot for his airs,' the king thought. 'But not this man. I need him too much. And so does the kingdom, for I do not doubt his loyalty to it.'

Ashoka knew that the Brahmin's commitment to

Magadha went beyond personal loyalty. It was a bond that would live even beyond his lifetime, as long as the kingdom existed.

'What is his hold over me?' the king wondered. As if in response to his unspoken question, the Brahmin looked up at his monarch with the conspiratorial affection of old comrades. The answer hit Ashoka in the pit of his stomach like a rush of air.

'Because he doesn't need anything from me!' He was the king of Magadha, the arbiter of vanquished kingdoms and the head of an army so powerful that nobody had seen the likes of it before, yet here was one man who did not need his favour. The realization made him feel small somehow. For a moment, he felt an intense dislike for the man standing in front of him. Then it passed.

The Brahmin clasped his hands behind his back and surveyed the great hall. It blazed with lights. Suspended close together on interwoven silver ropes were hundreds of glass lamps casting their iridescent glow across the ceiling that seemed to stretch endlessly. Below the royal dais, courtiers sat in a semicircle, in order of precedence. The ministers and the aristocrats, accompanied by their wives, were in front. Their ranks included the pradeshtri, head of the revenue and judicial service; the prashastri, minister of correspondence, whose task it was to draft decrees and royal letters; the dauvarika, chamberlain or master of ceremonies; the purohit, who was the royal spiritual advisor; and the senapati, or commander-in-chief, along with the admiral of the navy. Right behind them were the antapalas, the guardians of the frontiers, and the durgapalas, the commanders of forts, along with the viceroys of the provinces. In the same row were senior officials dressed in full regalia, magistrates, chiefs of police of various provinces and important excise and customs officials. Behind them was the row comprising the shresthins and their wives, dressed in their best finery; rich merchants and foreign traders. A separate section was reserved for one hundred and one brahmins and another for diplomats and foreign travellers. Soldiers with stout spears and huge wooden shields covered with oxhide protected the throne room. A group of battle-hardened Greeks, Magadhans, Gandharas and Kambojas formed a perimeter around Ashoka and Asandhimitra.

In the diplomatic section, Angyo and his armed monks stood at a slight distance behind Suma and Mur. The envoy looked nervous. Next to him, Mur, in a white satin dress and a string of luminous white pearls around her neck, wore a serene smile, as if none of this mattered to her. Hao kept close to the Brahmin, her eyes fixed on Mur and Suma.

'We do not like to be kept waiting, Brahmin,' the king snarled.

The spymaster cleared his throat and began, 'My story starts in an island kingdom in the south, where your friend Devanapriya is the king now. One of his ancestors several centuries ago was Ravana, a king renowned for his good looks, scholarship and magical powers. Unlike most kings, he was a brahmin. One day, while hunting in the forest, he saw a young woman and fell in love with her. Only, she happened to be the wife of Rama, the exiled prince of Ayodhya. Ravana kept her captive in a garden palace, called the Ashoka Vana – the forest of Ashoka.'

The king raised an eyebrow at the mention of his name.

The Brahmin went on unperturbed, 'One day, Rama came with a mighty army to rescue her. The war lasted thirteen days and nights. To Ravana's great grief, most of his sons and brothers were killed – except the treacherous Vibheeshana. But unknown to all, he had nine other brothers, who were brought up in secret by his father in the forest. He trusted them most of all, nine highly trained warriors who travelled across kingdoms to learn the secrets of other rulers and exterminated his enemies by stealth. and the secret nine in the forest, who had been ordered to stay away from the war and keep the affairs of the kingdom in order. They guarded his secrets as their own, for he was theirs. As hero after hero in his ranks fell, Ravana realised it was time to summon the them. By this time, both opponents had exhausted their magical weapons, but the war was not over yet. Ravana had one last weapon in his armoury – the Golden Scythe, the most powerful weapon of annihilation in the world, which Lord Shiva himself had given him. Ravana knew that if he used it, the world would be destroyed, and along with it, everything he held dear.

'On the last day of the war, Ravana gave the Scythe to the oldest of the nine, to guard with his life. When he died, it would pass on to his eldest son, and so on. The nine brothers fled into the forest and disappeared. Over time the legend of the Golden Scythe was forgotten.

'Centuries later, Buddhist monks came to Lanka. Attracted by their message of peace, people began to convert to their faith.'

'Where is the Scythe now? Are the monks hiding it?' Ashoka asked impatiently.

'A week ago,' said the Brahmin, 'Girika informed his friend Radhapupta about a weapon with the power to destroy the world. A young Buddhist monk from faraway Lanka had told him this, under duress. But before Girika could learn more, the monk died. His last words were about a Lankan princess who was on her way to Pataliputra to meet me. This got your prime minister thinking.'

'Radhagupta has already informed me about her, while you were keeping it a secret. He put two and two together and also guessed the princess had the Scythe with her,' Ashoka snapped. 'Where is she, and the weapon?'

'Rumour has it that the Brahmin knows where the princess is,' Radhagupta broke in.

'Apparently, so did Lord Suma,' Asandhimitra interjected. 'He was searching for her in our palace in Ujjain.'

Suma gave a pale smile. 'I was acting on rumours, Your Majesty, as the prime minister suggests,' he said.

Ashoka laughed mirthlessly. 'Do you and Radhapupta trade only in rumours? That's funny. After all those parleys about improving relations between our two countries, is that all you know? Mere hearsay?'

The Brahmin admired Ashoka's composure, which

gave nothing away, though his mind was consumed with vengeful hatred for Suma and all of Kalinga.

'Carry on with your story,' Ashoka said tersely.

'The nine brahmins in our story crossed the sea and landed in southern Bharatvarsha. Their unique skills made them invaluable spies in any king's court. They worked as secret agents, exposing threats, conspiracies, discovering hidden treasures and advising their masters on strategy in war and peace. They became the greatest masters of espionage of all time. But they kept in touch with each other, bonded for ever by the pact to keep the Scythe safe.'

The king fixed the Brahmin with a stony stare. 'Like you?'

'Yes, I too, sire. I am a descendant of that line.'

'You mean a clan of brahmins descended from Ravana are secret agents in all the great courts of the land? Who was there before you in Magadha?'

Before the Brahmin could open his mouth, understanding dawned in Ashoka's eyes. He slapped his thigh and the sound echoed through the vast room. People recoiled in their seats.

'Chanakya!' Ashoka roared. 'He was one of you, wasn't he?'

The Brahmin shrugged and continued, 'Now let me tell you another story, from a time closer to ours. Almost a century ago, a Greek king set out to conquer the world. His name was Alexander. He defeated all the empires that lay in his path, and entered the land of the Indus. A few years later, he turned back to Macedonia, compelled by his homesick soldiers. A descendant of the nine accompanied him. His name was Kalyan.'

'Kalanos of Taxila? Who joined Alexander's army on its way back home, and immolated himself at Sousa? He was a spy?' asked Asandhimitra.

'He was the spymaster of Porus,' the Brahmin said.

'After their defeat, Porus and his men had been brought in chains by the Greek soldiers to Alexander. Kalyan had fought by his king till the end and Alexander had noticed his bravery on the battlefield. As Kalyan stood before him, his gaze fell on the small golden cone encased in leaded glass around his neck. Its beauty and immaculate symmetry dazzled him. After he gave Porus his freedom, he asked for the cone as a gift. Kalyan had no choice but to obey. But he vowed that he would get it back and kill Alexander too.

'Over the months, as they travelled towards Macedonia, he impressed Alexander with his knowledge and statecraft and became part of his inner circle. Now, Alexander was obsessed with the idea of immortality and was convinced the holy men of Bharat held the key to it. Kalyan tricked him. He persuaded Alexander to remove the glass covering around the Scythe and give it to him for safe keeping. He then told the king that exposing the cone to the sun would release its power and with Apollo's blessings the Macedonian will become a god. The opposite happened.

'Go on.'

'Alexander was delighted. Kalyan knew that it was a matter of time before the king died and he got the

Scythe back. But then something happened which he hadn't anticipated.'

The Brahmin looked around, his eyes aflame with the fires of the past. The court seemed frozen in a tableau. Old ghosts were present. The Brahmin could feel them caressing his face with cold, trembling fingers whorled with anguished memories of things past – friendship, treachery and doomed love. Mur gathered her thin shawl about her slim white shoulders. Suma had shrunk into himself. Even Ashoka and his queen shifted uneasily on their thrones. Only the palace guards, including the grizzly old warrior to Ashoka's left, stood like stone statues, their shields and spears tightly gripped in muscular arms, sandalled feet firmly planted on the ground.

'What did Kalyan not foresee?' Asandhimitra asked softly.

'Loyalty,' replied the spymaster. 'The key to unravelling this mystery is loyalty. It's loyalty that drove the spymasters, enriched the friendship of kings and kept alive the allegiance to a cause taken up by a brotherhood several centuries ago. Loyalty that binds. Loyalty that destroys.'

'Stop your riddles, Brahmin.' Impatience seared Ashoka's voice.

'Your Majesty, what Kalyan did not anticipate was that a young Greek captain had overheard his conversation with Alexander. He followed Kalyan and watched as he concealed the case under a rock. When Alexander began to sicken, the captain suspected it was because of the cone. He wanted to warn Alexander but he knew that the king would not take the word of a mere soldier over that of a learned Brahmin warrior he trusted. Instead, he confronted Kalyan, who denied all knowledge of it. The captain then posted guards outside the royal tent, with orders to not let anyone in without his permission, except for Alexander's physicians and generals.

'One night, as an ailing Alexander lay asleep, the captain stole into his tent and removed the cone from around his neck. He put it back in the case that he had retrieved from where Kalyan had hidden it, and fled to Taxila. There, he would be safe among the many Greeks who had stayed back in the city.

'Meanwhile, Alexander lay dying, his stupor interrupted by brief moments of clarity. During one of these, he realised the cone was missing. Soldiers were sent out after the missing captain, but they soon returned after a futile search. The army was tired by now and looking for a lucky charm was not as important as seeing their wives and children again.

'Kalyan was devastated, knowing that the Scythe was lost to him for ever. He decided to immolate himself and told Alexander of his decision, without giving him a reason for it. Alexander tried to dissuade him, but he wouldn't budge. Before he took his seat on the pyre, he bade farewell to the commanders. But not to Alexander. Perhaps he was ashamed of his treachery, or the fact that life held no more meaning. He had betrayed an ancient oath. Before the pyre was lit, Kalyan told Alexander that they would meet again in Babylon. Strangely, the Macedonian died in Babylon a few months later.'

'So where is the Scythe now?' Ashoka asked, disturbed.

'One day, the young Greek captain told his wife the story of the Scythe. The frightened woman stole it when he was sleeping and fled with their child to a Buddhist monastery. She gave the abbot the weapon and expressed her desire to become a nun.'

'Then?'

'The captain, on discovering what his wife had done, stormed into the monastery. The abbott met him and took him to his chamber. When they came out, the captain announced his decision to join the monastery. But the abbott wouldn't let him.'

'Why not?' asked Asandhimitra, her eyes shining with interest.

'He ordered him to take the Golden Scythe to a certain brahmin serving in the court of the king of Lanka. Accompanied by his wife and son, the soldier travelled to Lankapuri, the island kingdom's capital. There, he handed over the Golden Scythe as directed. On the way back, a sickness took his wife and the grieving widower decided to go to Pataliputra with his little boy. There, he would seek employment in the king's army.'

'He must be dead by now,' Ashoka said. 'These events happened so many years ago.'

'But it was only recently that Lord Suma heard from his spies in Lanka about a princess arriving in Pataliputra with a precious gift.'

'The Golden Scythe! She was bringing it to me,' Ashoka said triumphantly.

The Brahmin shook his head. 'No, my lord, she was bringing it to me. In the secret world of spies, the whispers had begun to gather strength, of the legend of the Scythe and its destructive powers. General Nandidevi's men traced it back to Lanka and tried to steal it. But my brother, who was King Devanapriya's chief spy, foiled their plans. He was grievously injured in the scuffle. Before he died, he advised the king to send the Scythe to me. The king then sent it to me through his daughter, his only child, for safekeeping. There was no one else he could trust with it.'

The Brahmin looked up at Ashoka. 'I am the last of the line,' he said.

Ashoka's eyes grew feverish.

'So you have it, Brahmin,' he exclaimed, holding out his hand.

'I did have it, Your Majesty, but not any more.'

The Terrible Truth

Ashoka glowered at the Brahmin. A storm gathered on his wide forehead and his lips drew back in a snarl – a beast cheated of its prize.

Where is the princess? Find her!' he roared.

'Patience, my lord. Listen to rest of the story, please. After a long journey, the Lankan princess reached Pataliputra with the Golden Scythe. She realized that the best place to hide until she found me was in the harem, where access was restricted. Then she bribed the Chief Eunuch to let her in and arrange a meeting with me. Sensing an opportunity, the Chief Eunech contacted Radhagupta, who asked him if the girl had a birthmark on her forearm. The eunuch began to blackmail the princess over the birthmark, telling her that Radhagupta's spies in the harem were looking for her. The princess realised she could hold off the eunuch with money for some time but she had to find me quickly, before she was exposed. She also surmised there must be Kalingan spies in the palace. And she was right, because Suma had his agents everywhere. So she looked for a harem girl who resembled her the most and bribed her to get a tattoo on her arm, just like the birthmark. When the Chief Eunuch realised what she had done, he told Radhagupta that there were two girls in the harem with similar birthmarks and asked for gold to bring the right girl to him. Meanwhile, Suma ordered the Blood

Flower to find and kill the princess, and seize the Scythe. Disguised as a concubine, the assassin entered the palace grounds and was shocked to hear from Suma's spies that a girl had been found dead at the cremation ground. A girl with a birthmark on her partially charred hand.'

'You mean my concubine was killed by someone else?' asked Ashoka.

'The Blood Flower had no means to tell if the dead girl was the princess. Only the Chief Eunuch could, but he had gone missing from the prison. Then a further complication rose. A strange woman had appeared in the harem wearing black gloves and established herself as the protector of the other girl with the birthmark. This was a setback to the Blood Flower.'

'How could a man get into a heavily guarded harem to kill one of the concubines?' interrupted Asandhimitra.

'A man could not, Your Majesty. But a woman could,' replied the Brahmin.

'A woman?' Asandhimitra gasped.

'Yes. A woman called the Blood Flower.' The Brahmin turned and pointed at Mur. 'She has been trained by the best of Nandidevi's spymasters, fighters, sorcerers, surgeons, illusionists and poisoners to be Kalinga's single most dangerous weapon.'

At a gesture from the Brahmin, Angyo and his monks encircled Mur. She kept her gaze fixed on a distant lamp on the celling, as if she hadn't heard.

'Dao,' Hao sighed. 'Oh, Dao.'

Suma protested loudly. A look from the king silenced him. 'How can you be certain Mur is the Blood Flower?' Ashoka asked the Brahmin.

'When I first met her, at the inn on the road to Ujjain, she seemed glad to see me. I made the mistake of presuming that a girl riding with ruffians would welcome better company even though I was sure she was a Kalingan spy. I was sure I would be able to keep a watch on her. My vanity was my failing. The innkeeper drugged my wine at her behest. The last thing I remembered was something being tossed at me as she was leaving. After Angyo rescued me, I found it under a bench. It was a kovidara, a blood flower. That's when I realized who Mur was.'

'So, was the girl you passed off as a poor lord's daughter really one? The girl who was murdered in the Ujjain palace?' Suma asked sarcastically.

'Once the concubine was killed, the princess knew she had to find me, and find me fast. She had learned that Antochlius was in my employ; there are few secrets in a harem. The princess requested him to take her to me. It was a brief meeting. I asked Antochlius to accompany her to Ujjain the same night, where she would be safe with Her Majesty. To confuse any pursuers, I asked Antochlius to procure a girl who resembled the princess to go with her. He found a dancing girl. On their way to the Office of Secrets, they found the corpse of the Chief Eunuch. Antochlius had previously discovered that the princess was in the company of a woman wearing black gloves. He took her too, to Ujjain, with the girls. How the dancer got the mark on her arm, I can only guess,' he said, smiling at the queen. Asandhimitra did not smile back.

'And the princess?' Ashoka asked.

'On the way to Ujjain, Telemachus and Suma's men ambushed Antochlius. There he made his last stand, urging the princess to flee to Ujjain.'

'Who killed the Chief Eunuch then?'

The Brahmin shrugged. 'The Chief Eunuch was blackmailing Radhagupta and Suma. He had become a liability because he knew too much.'

Hao's gaze was fixed on Mur with fierce intensity. The king gazed thoughtfully at the prime minister, who was shifting in his seat. Then he swerved his gaze to the Brahmin and his fist came down hard on the arm of the throne.

'You, spymaster, after six days, haven't solved a single murder or found the Golden Scythe. It's not mere talk I need, but the princess. Find her, Brahmin, or else you need not come back to my court ever.'

'I did find her, but she is not in Magadha any more. She is back home, with her father. She was afraid, this daughter of King Devanapriya. She told me everything, of my brother's murder, her father's aversion to violence as a Buddhist and his resolve to send the Golden Scythe to me.'

Ashoka pointed a stern finger at the Brahmin. 'You mean, you have it?'

'I seek your indulgence for a few minutes more, great Ashoka,' said the Brahmin, with a trace of mockery.

'Are you playing with me, spymaster? If you are, I'll have your head smashed to pulp by elephants!'

'Antochlius, though he was my spy, also had Queen

Asandhimitra's ear. Perhaps she sent one of her own spies to Pataliputra to protect the princess – perhaps, the woman wearing the black gloves. I learnt it was this woman who threatened the Chief Eunuch with dire punishment if he played Suma and Radhagupta's game. It was to her that I gave the Scythe for safekeeping, after the princess handed it over to me. And now, she has it.'

The spymaster turned towards the queen and bowed. Mischief played on his face. Ashoka looked at Asandhimitra in shock.

Asandhimitra clapped her hands and smiled.

'Bravo, spymaster! You have excelled yourself,' she said.

Wordlessly Ashoka held out his hand. Surprise and suspicion played on his face. Asandhimitra called to Hao. The Viet girl shook her head as if she was coming up for air, and reluctantly shifted her gaze from Mur. From the pocket of her pantaloons, she took out a small, plain wooden box and gave it to the queen.

'I passed this on to her while we were hiding,' the queen explained, taking the box. 'The Brahmin gave it to me before he sent us off to that secret room you never told me about.' The last part of her sentence was addressed to Ashoka in a caustic tone. The king looked momentarily discomfited. Asandhimitra opened the box and gently took out a shining cone in a glass case. The Golden Scythe emitted a low hum, pulsing with a merciless light of its own, almost blinding anyone who set eyes upon it. It rippled with dark, deep shadows and unnamed forces. Its energy field charged the atmosphere, shining like life in all its beauty. And like death in all its savage glory.

Ashoka sat frozen on his throne. Slowly, he reached out and took the cone from Asandhimitra. His eyes blazed with triumph. Lord Suma was slumped in his chair. All the life seemed to have drained out of him.

Ashoka clapped the Brahmin on his shoulder.

'Did you give him permission to leave, Your Majesty?' Hao's voice suddenly rang out. She had one arm around Radhagupta's neck, while the other hand held a dagger to his throat. At a signal from the Brahmin, Hao removed the dagger and Radhagupta collapsed at Ashoka's feet, sobbing uncontrollably.

'The Brahmin is lying,' he cried.

Ashoka shook his head.

'No, he has witnesses who have recorded your meetings with Suma, your affair with the traitor Telemachus and your conspiracy against Magadha. How dare you?'

At a signal from the king, the palace guards dragged away the disgraced official, who left struggling and screaming obscenities against the Brahmin.

'I have all the proof necessary to show Lord Suma's involvement in the plot to harm the queen and take the Golden Scythe,' the Brahmin said, 'including the death of Devavarman. Unfortunately he is a guest of Magadha, and a diplomat who enjoys protection from prosecution.'

Suma sprang up, his chest puffed out like a bony pigeon's. He had regained some of his old confidence.

'I didn't know Mur was an assassin,' he declared. 'She is just the daughter of a distant cousin. All I knew was, she was to marry Devavarman. How could I know that she would kill him?'

'We didn't say she did, so why do you suggest it?' the Brahmin asked.

'You speak nonsense, Brahmin,' Suma blustered.

The spymaster pulled out the retrieved war plans from the pocket of his tunic and flung them at Suma's feet.

'Mur did kill him, Suma, for these. She seduced him first and then killed him for the king's war plans. We got them back, drafted new ones with some changes and put them back where you had hidden them. The war plans you sent to Nandidevi were fakes.'

Suma looked as if he had been slapped.

'You tried and failed, Suma. In this game only one man can win,' the Brahmin said contemptuously.

He heard a swift movement behind him and whirled around. His eyes went to the circle of soldiers guarding the king, coming to rest on the tall, lean, powerful looking guard to Ashoka's left. His skin showed the welts and scars of many battles. Only his iron-gray hair betrayed his age. It was cut short to his skull, and barely showed below his iron helmet. His neat beard was clipped close to his chin. His eyes burned with rage. The Brahmin started towards him, but the soldier moved quickly, shoving aside the guard standing nearest him with a strong elbow to create space for his right arm as he pulled out a dagger from his belt.

'Seize him, he is the one who murdered the girls!' the Brahmin called out.

'For Antochlius!' the old man screamed.

Before anyone could grab him, he flung the dagger. The Brahmin's reflexes caused him to bend backward just in time, as a spit of air passed above him in the wake of its passage. The world slowed down. Hao moved with almost invisible speed, flinging herself in the dagger's path to protect the king and the queen. But it was not meant for them. It flew true and straight with lethal aim towards Mur.

With an eye-defying movement, the Blood Flower tilted away from her seat like a flowing sprite and reached forward to grasp the incoming dagger by its hilt. Later, those present would speak in awe of the young woman who was one moment a beautiful creature lounging in her seat, and the next a white blur of dazzling speed. She spun around and launched the dagger at the king. Before anyone could react, Hao moved again and took the knife in her shoulder. As she staggered back, her arm flashed in an arc and the Brahmin saw Mur's red mouth open wide, blood spewing from it. She had doubled up in shock, her eyes wide and dark. She opened her mouth in a wordless cry, clutching the hilt of the dagger embedded in her chest; the dagger Hao had pulled out of her own shoulder and hurled at her. Her eyes grew very large, then she collapsed on the ground.

'Antochlius has been avenged at last!' the old soldier cried in triumph.

Soldiers tried to grab him as he made a dash for the door. They flung themselves on him, dragging him to the floor. Once he was subdued, they bound his hands behind his back. Ashoka was frozen in shock. Asandhimitra had risen from her throne, white-faced and trembling. Her left hand gripped Ashoka's forearm tightly. He gently disengaged himself and drew her to him. The soldiers dragged the old warrior forward and forced him down on his knees before Ashoka.

The Brahmin walked across to Mur and felt for a pulse in her neck. She lay like a fallen white flower in an expanding pool of blood. Her black hair, unbound, fanned out like a dark wave stilled by enchantment.

Ashoka looked at the old soldier struggling to break free from his captors. It took five men to hold the giant down.

'Don't you recognize him, Your Majesty?' asked the Brahmin. 'Don't you recognize Aeimnestus, father of Antochlius and the man who took the Golden Scythe from Kalanos?'

'I do now. He is our loyal subject who fought many wars alongside my grandfather and my father. I gave him a job in the palace after he became too old to fight. His son Antochlius was one of the best of my bodyguards until he was murdered.' He glanced at Suma meaningfully.

Suma's diplomatic composure was gone. The Brahmin saw him as he really was: a small, cunning man steeped in arrogance, greed and cruelty.

'This is unpardonable,' Suma shouted. 'In the king's own court, my niece slain by one of the king's own assassins.'

Ashoka stared at Suma, his powerful gaze cowing the diplomat into servile silence. The king's power dominated the room, like a great tiger about to pounce on its prey.

'We are truly sorry for what happened to your niece,' Ashoka said grimly.

He turned to the Brahmin and ordered that Mur's body be taken away.

Aeimnestus wept kneeling before Ashoka, all the fight gone out of him. His grief touched the hearts of the haughty, powerful men and women of Ashoka's court, reminding them of their own mortality.

'I have failed you. Alexander,' Aeimnestus keened inconsolably, rocking on his haunches. 'I failed you, Antochlius.'

With a last powerful heave of his muscled arms, he flung back the guards. He grabbed a sword from the nearest man's war belt and fell on it, his face twisting in a grimace of pain. His widening eyes were filled with sadness and regret. Slowly, he keeled over to one side, gave a great sigh and died.

'The price of loyalty is high,' the Brahmin remarked softly. 'He killed the girls for nothing.'

'How did he do it?' asked Asandhimitra.

'Who notices a soldier among a score of soldiers?' the Brahmin asked, his hand sweeping the air, indicating the guards who ringed the throne room. 'They are everywhere, taken for granted as permanent fixtures. Coincidentally, Aeimnestus was drinking in a tavern where he overheard Radhagupta, Suma and the Chief Eunuch discussing the Scythe and the princess with a birthmark. He knew he couldn't identify the princess, so he blackmailed the eunuch by threatening to reveal his trysts with the traitors unless he brought her to him. The eunuch brought the concubine to the cremation ground where Aeimnestus was waiting. Why he chose the cremation ground nobody knows; perhaps because it was far away from the palace where he would have been recognized. When he questioned the girl, all she could tell him was that she was planning to go to Ujjain. Realizing she was not the princess, he killed her to avoid being found out. Then he joined the cavalry escort to Ujjain, where he waited for a chance to get at the princess and grab the Golden Scythe.'

'All this, for loyalty to the dead Alexander?' Ashoka remarked.

'Loyalty is a double-edged sword, Your Majesty. Its enemy is not betrayal, but love.'

'Ah, what I would give for someone as loyal to me as Aeimnestus was to his king!' Ashoka sighed. 'You have done well, Brahmin.'

Ashoka gripped the Golden Scythe tightly in his hands, as if it contained the essence of his dark soul. He turned to his queen. His brow was clouded, but his eyes were surprisingly gentle. The Brahmin saw the look that passed between them, and realized the strength of their bond.

'I have questions for you, my queen,' Ashoka said. 'But later.'

Asandhimitra inclined her head gracefully, a soft smile teasing her lips. Ashoka turned to the Brahmin.

'I knew my trust in you was not misplaced. Ask for anything you want, and I'll grant your wish.'

The Brahmin bowed. 'I seek permission to leave your service,' he answered.

'Leave me?' Ashoka roared in anger. 'You have ensured

the dominance of Magadha over the world and you want to leave me? Your work here is not finished yet!'

'I will be back one day,' the Brahmin said. 'When the war is over.'

'Which war?' Ashoka's eyes twinkled with cruel mischief.

The spymaster smiled thinly. He looked at those gathered in the hall. His eyes came to rest on Hao and became uncharacteristically gentle. She had fashioned a crude bandage with her tunic to stem the blood from her shoulder wound. Tears ran down her cheeks, though her face remained expressionless, as if a stranger had taken her place while she was lost in mourning. Worry clouded the Brahmin's eyes. He watched as she stepped over the fallen Aeimnestus and approached Mur where she lay. Her shoulders shivered, as if she was very cold. She sat down beside Mur's corpse, and gently placed her head on her lap. Stroking her cheeks and hair, she began to rock back and forth, wailing silently as if all the demons of hell were screaming in torment within her breast. The Brahmin started forward, but the queen stopped him.

'Let her be, spymaster,' she said quietly. 'I can see she is mourning someone she loved. Even though it was an assassin.'

Ashoka looked at Suma thoughtfully for a long moment.

'What should I do with you, ambassador?'

'You have to set me free because I am the rightful envoy of Kalinga and am protected by the laws of diplomacy. You cannot kill me.'

'Kill you? Of course not! How will I pass on my message to your boy-king that Magadha cannot be trifled with?'

He gestured to the guards to seize Suma. 'Blind him. Cut off his hands and feet, slice off his ears and nose. But leave his tongue, because I need him to tell Susruta that Magadha is coming,' he ordered.

Ashoka got up and held his hand out to the queen. Taking it as a gesture of dismissal, the court rose.

Asandhimitra disengaged her hand from Ashoka's clasp and went up to the Brahmin.

'Mur and Hao are sisters, aren't they? The resemblance is striking,' she said softly.

The Brahmin looked up, startled. How could he have missed it? Mur's make up and rich clothes had misdirected him from guessing the truth. He recalled Radhagupta's accusation that the woman who had spirited the Chief Eunuch out of Girika's clutches had Hao's eyes. The Blood Flower had freed him, hoping he would lead her to the princess. And he almost had.

'I saw Hao pick up the veil in the Garden of Secrets the night the Chief Eunuch was killed. You will never have a better friend or ally,' Asandhimitra said.

'You were in the garden?' the Brahmin asked. Suddenly things fell into place.

'You did a brave thing, Your Majesty,' he said.

'All I wanted was to keep the king and the kingdom safe. And also that little girl.'

'And get the Scythe.'

'That too,' she said. 'Ashoka needs it now more than

ever. His enemies are gathering like vultures. Some of our own generals wish to see him dead, so that the kingdom will crumble and they can carve out their own little fiefdoms. But one day Ashoka will be emperor, and that will put an end to their dreams.'

She placed a soft hand on his shoulder. The Buddha bangle on her arm glistened.

'He needs this war, and you know it. We cannot let him down.'

'You played your role well, my Queen,' the Brahmin said softly, his glance going to the gold ornament glinting on her wrist, 'You wore black gloves to hide this, not a birthmark, didn't you?'

Without a word, the queen left the room with Ashoka, who was impatiently waiting for her, but the Brahmin did not know how to comfort her. He had never cried himself.

Epilogue

Hao slept with her head on the Brahmin's shoulder. He listened to the rhythm of her breathing and the beating of her heart. The wound on her shoulder had healed, but he knew it would take years for the wound within her to heal.

If ever.

While recuperating in the monastery, Hao had told him about her and Dao, twin sisters orphaned in the war between the forces of Viet Land's young Lady Triêu and the Chinese state of Eastern Wu. Triêu had become a bandit queen with a company of over a thousand men. Hao would often quote her famous saying, 'I want to ride storms, kill sharks in the open sea, drive out the aggressors, reconquer the country, undo the ties of serfdom, and never bend my back to be the concubine of any man.'

The twins had grown up in a village in Cúu Chân district, daughters of a rich merchant. One day, the Chinese attacked the village and burned it down. They killed all the old men and women. The able-bodied men were taken as slaves, and the women were either sold to procurers or raped and sold in the open market. The children, too, became slaves. Dao managed to escape from her captors. However, Hao was sold to a tavern keeper, whom she later killed with a kitchen knife, when he tried to rape her. She fled to the forest like her heroine, Triêu, and gathered a gang of her own. They lived in the forest, preying on merchant caravans and the entourages of court officials.

One day, she was betrayed by a member of her gang and caught by the Chinese, who ordered her execution. Fortunately for her, Viet rebels attacked the town in Phú Điên where she was imprisoned, and she managed to escape again. Exhausted, she stopped at a monastery of warrior monks. The abbot took to her as if she was his own daughter. Under him, she studied the art of fighting, the ways of deception and the science of healing. But her peaceful days did not last very long. The Chinese army, commanded by Lu Yin, the inspector of Jiaozhou, with orders to crush the resistance after Lady Triêu's revolt, arrived at the monastery and put it to the torch because the abbot wouldn't bow before them. Hao was captured again, but not before she had killed over two dozen seasoned warriors. This brought her to Lu Yin's attention. He trained her to become a spy and an assassin. He also took her as his mistress.

Hao escaped again, and travelled through plains and mountains, villages and cities, palaces and taverns, looking for Dao. She lent her services to local chieftains on the way, fighting, looting and killing for her temporary masters. She found traces of Dao here and there. Through the wide network of contacts made during her travels and adventures, she heard rumours of a beautiful Viet assassin named the Blood Flower, who looked eerily like her; a skilful murderess, wily and swift, who disappeared without leaving a trace after carrying out her mission.

Whenever a palace official was found drowned in his bath or a nobleman's garroted corpse was discovered with a dead whore in a back alley or a rebellious prince was shot down by a ghost archer in broad daylight while hunting with his falcons, a name was spoken in awe – the Blood Flower. Few had seen her. Nobody knew her.

One day, while Hao was sleeping in a garret on top of a wine house where she was working as a serving wench, her sixth sense woke her. Someone was nearby. In a flash she raised her hips and swivelled around, lashing out with her feet. Immediately she was pinned down and a laughing face with dancing eyes and crimson mouth confronted her. Hao felt she was looking in a mirror.

'Dao?' she whispered.

The visitor nodded, but did not release her grip. She bent down, kissed Hao on her forehead and whispered, 'Dao is dead, my love. Now there is only the Blood Flower. I go by many names. Do not look for me anymore. You won't find me. Life has set us on different paths, sister, and it has changed us both. If you still love Dao's memory, as she was to you in childhood, promise me you'll not look for her.'

Through the film of her tears, Hao saw the sadness in her sister's eyes, mixed with fierce determination. Time and fate had changed them both. Hao nodded. She never saw the blow coming, but when she woke up with a headache that would collapse an elephant, Dao had vanished.

The Brahmin felt her stir beside him and tried to get up. Hao held him tightly.

'Not yet, I'm still sleepy,' she murmured, and added sardonically, 'Master.'

The twilight floated in through the vaulted windows of the monastery. A bird cried in the orchard below and the wind visited their chamber, bringing the scent of oranges. The Brahmin heard the clash of steel, the blows of stout staffs, loud grunts and cries from outside. He smiled to himself. They never stopped, the warrior monks of Tamralipti.

During the past few weeks, since they had arrived at the monastery accompanied by Angyo and his fighters, the Brahmin had watched over Hao as she tossed and turned in drug induced stupor while her wounds healed. He heard her call out to Dao, weeping uncontrollably. All the while, through the day and night, the warrior monks practiced their art in the courtyard below. Somehow, the sounds of fighting were comforting. The Brahmin had sat by Hao for days, like he had many years ago beside his wounded prince, waiting for him to heal. Until one evening, he felt a pair of cool, fair arms encircle his neck and a small head bury itself in his chest.

The Brahmin's thoughts were interrupted by a soft knock at the door. Two men entered. One was Angyo. The other man was cowled, and dressed in a deep crimson robe. His face was shadowed, but the Brahmin remembered him like a vision from a distant dream; eyes like lamps and a voice so gentle and hypnotic that it felt like the pull of the tide of an endless ocean.

'Master?' he whispered.

The figure gently walked up to them, and laid a hand on Hao.

'She has recovered,' he said. 'Though it will take some time for her to be healed. The monks have done their work well.'

'You made a promise,' said Angyo.

'I remember,' the Brahmin said.

He got up from his palliasse and went over to his baldric, which was hanging on the wall. He fished inside its pocket and brought out a small bundle of cloth. Angyo held out his hand. The Brahmin shook his head.

'I wish to give it to him myself,' he said.

He stepped up to the Master and offered him the bundle reverentially. The Master handed his staff to Angyo and received it in his hand. As he opened it, a great light spread through the room, filling it with a sense of deep calm. He held up a golden cone, identical to the one the spymaster had given Ashoka.

'The Golden Scythe,' Angyo whispered.

'There are two of them,' the Master said. 'The Scythe of Peace and the Scythe of War. You know which one this is.'

The spymaster bowed his head. The Master laughed. It sounded like a silver bell tinkling in a pasture through which a stream ran, gurgling.

'You gave the Scythe of Peace to Ashoka,' the Master said. 'And you brought the other one to me.'

'Ashoka would have gone to war, with or without the Scythe, and conquered Kalinga,' the Brahmin said. 'The Scythe of War would have damned the empire and his soul, and the world with it. I hope that the influence of the Scythe of Peace will change his bloodthirsty nature and make him a great king.'

'It will,' said the Master. 'I thank you. Now it's time for me to take this with me to a place where it will never be found, or recognized. You have done us a great service.'

He touched the Brahmin's head. The spymaster felt the sky open within him, the universe expanding, racing him through galaxies and the luminescence of supernovas as he was pulled towards eternity.

'Who are you?' he whispered.

'Who I am is not of any consequence. I am a traveller like you,' the Master said. 'I was a prince once. They called me Rahula of Kapilavastu. I started my journey from the northern mountains, looking for my lost father, but in the end I found myself.'

After the Master left, Angyo drew the Brahmin to him and held him in a tight embrace.

'Thank you, brother,' he said. 'Thank you for saving us all. Please feel free to stay in the monastery for as long as you like. This is a healing place.'

The Brahmin looked at Hao. She shook her head. There would be other kings to serve, more battles to be fought and mysteries to be unravelled. There would always be intrigue, murder and betrayal.

I'm engaged in a race with evil, the Brahmin thought. Sometimes I reach the spot before it does and sometimes only after it has left, spilling blood. But I will always be there. Like the nine who came first.

Hao smiled at him, her face illuminated with incandescent emotion. His eyes softened. He held out his hands. A small sigh escaped her, like sorrow leaving. She folded into his embrace and he gently stroked her hair.

'Come, my she-wolf,' the spymaster of Magadha said softly. 'Our horses are waiting.'

They saluted Angyo and walked out into the day. They did not see the cloaked figure in the shadows raise his hand in an unspoken blessing. Hao looked back.

'What?' the Brahmin asked.

'It was nothing,' Hao said with a smile. 'I thought I smelt flowers.'

Garuda tossed his massive head, neighing and pawing at the ground with steel-tipped hooves.

'Where to?' Hao asked.

'The road will tell us,' the Brahmin said as he nudged the great warhorse forward.

A long, slim cloud floated across the lazily rising sun, casting its shadow on earth. The sky winked.

ACKNOWLEDGEMENTS

I was inspired by the fascinating historical thrillers of Paul Doherty, Rory Clements, S.J. Parris and C.J. Sansom to write this book. *Ashoka: The Search for India's Lost Emperor* by Charles Allen and *Chandragupta* by Rajat Pillai provided some excellent details about the Maurya empire. I have taken some liberties with the dress, customs and architecture of the period, but have tried to be as accurate as possible in all other aspects.

My sincere gratitude to my publisher and editor, V.K. Karthika, for unravelling so many Gordian knots in the book. Also to Somak Ghosal for his astute editorial suggestions, Sapna Kapur and Nilanjan Das for their visual advice, and Pradyut Seal for his patience and creativity in rendering the cover illustration.